Evie

PEGGY DILLEY

Claremore, Oklahoma

Evie
Copyright © 2021 Peggy Dilley

Scripture quotations are from the King James Version of the Bible

All Rights Reserved. No part of this publication may be reproduced or transmitted in any form or by any means, electronic or mechanical, including photocopying and recording, or by any information storage and retrieval system, without prior written permission of the publisher. The only exception is brief quotations in printed or electronic reviews.

Cover photography copyright © 2021 Jim Dilley

The characters and events portrayed in this book are fictional, and any resemblance to actual persons or events is coincidental.

Published by Innovative Media, LLC
www.innovative-media.tv/publishing

Library of Congress Control Number: 2021947778

ISBN 978-1-7379483-0-8

Dedication

To my darling husband, Jim and our precious daughters, Keri, Aimee, and Amber. Thank you for your love and encouragement.

Chapter 1

It was 1946, after the war. Times were hard for everybody. We didn't have it as hard as some though. We only had three mouths to feed: Daddy, Mama, and me.

We had a little farm outside of Peoria, Illinois. Daddy worked hard to put food on the table. Everything was going just fine for us, until that dreadful day in May. May 17 to be exact.

Daddy was out plowing the fields. He figured all fear of frost was over for the year, and he was eager to get started on the crops. Trouble was, Daddy didn't come home for dinner like he always did. Mama had cooked up a pot of purple-hulled peas, cornbread, and fried potatoes. I was anxious for Daddy to come home. I was hungry, but more than anything I wanted some of the Johnny cakes Mama had made up for dessert.

I was only 14 years old, but something told me something just wasn't right. Mama must have felt it too because she kept wringing her hands, looking out the window.

Finally, she decided to find Daddy and tell him dinner was ready. So, she set out to the fields. I waited on the porch, eager for the uneasy feeling to go away, but it got a million times worse because I heard Mama scream—a scream I'm sure could be heard all the way up to heaven.

I saw Mama running back to the house. She threw herself on the ground and cried the most pitiful cry anyone could imagine. This behavior was so unnatural for Mama. She was usually so prim and proper. It scared me something awful to see Mama carrying on like that. I ran over and put my arms around her. She looked at me and cried harder. I was tempted to go to Daddy, but even my young mind reasoned that Daddy was the reason Mama was crying so.

Finally, Mama spoke, but her words didn't sound like her normal voice.

"Run on down to Leonard Smith's house!" Mama demanded in a strained, sad voice. "Tell him your mama needs help! Tell him it is very important that he comes soon."

I opened my mouth to ask Mama a question, but she held up her hand and cut me off before I could say a word. "Please, Evie! Don't ask me any questions, just go!"

I was never asked to do anything like this before. I wasn't even sure in which direction Leonard Smith lived. All of our neighbors lived so far apart from each other. But I knew

Evie

I had to find his house for Mama and Daddy. I took off running in the direction I thought best, and I guess I was right because Mama didn't call me back.

I ran as fast as my shaky legs could go. I have never felt so scared in all my life. Why did Mama need help? Something awful must have happened. Finally, I spotted the house, but it was still quite a way down the road. I had to stop and rest a bit. My lungs burned so bad I felt like they were going to burst wide open. I bent over and put my hands on my knees. I was breathing so hard I felt my whole body shaking. I stood up and noticed a truck coming down the road. Could it be? Yes, it looked to be Leonard Smith himself. He drove on past me but must have noticed that it was unusual for me to be all the way down the road by myself.

He pulled the truck over, got out, and asked, "Missy, what are you doing all the way up here?"

I could barely get the words out. I was still plum out of breath. "Mama sent me! She needs your help. She said it was real important!"

Leonard's face grew worried. He was a kind old man. His wife's name was Opal. They were a funny couple. He was tall and skinny, and she was short and fat. I told Mama that once and she scolded me. But then I caught her smiling and figured she thought they were funny too.

"Climb on up here. Let's go see what your mama needs," Leonard said in a strong voice. As we drove down the road, he asked me if Mama and Daddy were sick.

"I don't know," I answered. "Daddy didn't come in from the fields, so Mama went after him. She came back by herself crying."

Leonard stepped on the gas hard. We were going about as fast as the truck could go. Gravel was flying everywhere. I had to hold on to the seat to keep from falling into the floorboard.

Leonard drove right up into our yard. He jumped out of the truck. Mama was sitting on the porch step with her face in her hands.

"What's wrong, Laura?" Leonard asked with concern in his voice.

Mama fell into his arms and cried. She started saying something over and over, but I couldn't understand what she was saying. I realized later I did hear some of what she said. I just couldn't accept what she was saying. It was easier to pretend that I couldn't understand her because then maybe her words would not be true. Leonard took Mama by the arm and motioned for me to follow. He helped us both into his old truck and drove off to his house.

Evie

As we pulled up into Leonard's yard, Opal opened the screen door. She had a puzzled look on her face. Leonard told us to wait here because he would be right back. He ran over to Opal whispered something in her ear. She let out a gasp and then ran over to the truck. Leonard was by her side. He opened the door and helped Mama and me out of the truck. Opal pulled Mama into her chest and Mama just cried and cried.

Opal looked at me and said, "Come on, sweet thing." She pulled me into her chest.

Miss Opal's chest was big enough for both Mama and me. Finally, I guess everything caught up to me—the fast winded run, realizing that Daddy was probably dead. I let myself cry into Miss Opal's chest too. As she rubbed my back, she kept saying over and over, "You poor dear; you poor dear."

Leonard cleared his throat and said, "I'm going to go into town and fetch Doc. Hamilton and the sheriff. "Opal, why don't you take Laura and Evie on in the house and let them get cleaned up and rest a bit."

He then turned and left with a stern look on his face.

Mama then looked at me and asked Opal if she could have a little time alone with me. Miss Opal said sure, and she told us just to let ourselves in the house whenever we got ready. She gave us another sympathetic look, rubbed Mama's arm, and walked slowly through the screen door. I felt that once

5

Miss Opal was inside of the house, she would peer at us through the window, and I was right. There she was, right in the picture window, looking at us and wiping her eyes.

Mama guided me over to the Smith's porch. She pulled me down on her lap like I was a little girl again. She held my face to look square into hers. Even though I knew Mama was getting ready to tell me something awful, I couldn't help thinking that Mama had the prettiest blue eyes in the world. Daddy always told her that. Only now those beautiful blue eyes were filled with tears.

"Evie," Mama began, "something has happened to your daddy, something bad. Your daddy has died. He is in the arms of Jesus now."

When Mama said those words, I nodded my head in agreement, letting Mama know I already knew that information. What I didn't know, and what I wanted to know, was *how* Daddy died, but I just couldn't bring myself to ask. I just held Mama's hand and let my tears fall with her tears.

Chapter 2

The funeral was mighty sad. People were crying and hugging me and Mama. What really got me puzzled was trying to figure out how in the world the new preacher knew enough about Daddy to say all those kind words about him. He just kept going on and on about what a good man Daddy was. I knew he didn't know a lick about Daddy.

I never was told outright what happened to Daddy, but from what I heard other people saying, Daddy's heart stopped working and he fell off the tractor. They said the plow on the tractor just did him in good. It's what I heard some of the men saying at Daddy's funeral. They said there just wasn't enough of Daddy left to fix so he could look presentable at the funeral. So, between Mama, the doctor, and the undertaker, they decided to keep the casket closed.

It was ok with me. I didn't much want to see Daddy all in pieces. Besides, I had the good sense to know it wasn't Daddy in that casket anyway. Daddy had taken a trip to heaven.

He always said that we were all going there, some sooner than others. Daddy just beat Mama and me there, that's all.

Mama drove Daddy's truck back home after the funeral and stalled it about six times just trying to get home. Daddy had taught her to drive in case she ever needed to. Mama was never much good at it, but now was the time Mama needed to drive. Sweat was pouring down her face. She was so nervous. Her light brown curls were wet with sweat and sticking to her neck like little brown worms.

"Mama, are you ok?" I asked, feeling really worried about her.

"Yes, Evie, I'm just having a hard time getting this old pickup of your Daddy's to work right. How in the world people get these things to go without stopping, I don't know."

Finally, Mama got the thing working again and we pulled into the yard.

Mama and me walked into the house hand in hand. The house smelled the same and looked the same, but it didn't feel the same. The best way I could describe the feeling was empty. Mama must have felt the same way because she went off into the bedroom, shut the door, and cried. I think she cried all through the night.

Evie

Considering Mama cried through the night, I was surprised to smell and hear the crackling of bacon the next morning as I lay in bed. I jumped up and went into kitchen. Mama was dressed neatly as always. She only had three dresses: a Sunday dress and two everyday dresses, which were always ironed. And she always had her hair fixed. This morning, Mama had pinned her light brown curls back. Mama's eyes looked sad, but she was still real pretty. Daddy always said she was the prettiest woman he ever laid eyes on.

Mama looked at me and smiled—not one of Mama's real smiles, but a fake one. She was trying really hard to make things seem normal for me. Truth is, nothing would ever seem normal again, not without Daddy around. But I sure was glad she wasn't crying anymore.

I remember Mama's last real smile. It was the morning before Daddy died. I went into the kitchen, and they were both holding their coffee cups. They were smiling at each other. I heard them laugh. Just looking at them loving each other and having fun together made me feel loved.

Things were different now. It would just be Mama and me. I determined right then and there to keep letting Mama know how much she was loved. I went over and put my arms around her. She held me tight for a minute, and then she told me to sit down and eat my breakfast before it got cold.

Mama and I sat down to breakfast and ate in silence. We were both lost in our thoughts. My thoughts were on school. I only had two more weeks and then I would be off for the summer. I don't know where Mama's thoughts were. She sat at the table trying to be strong, but she looked mighty worried.

Chapter 3

It was now summer. Me and Mama were working real hard trying to keep the farm going. We had a little white house that Daddy said was not fancy but sound. I loved our little house. The house had a porch all across the front. The front door opened into a long hallway, and to the left of the hall was a door leading into Mama's kitchen. I loved the way the kitchen smelled: like cinnamon and baked bread. The sitting room was to the right of the hall, across from the kitchen. It was so cozy with Mama's knitted doilies all over, and fresh daisies in a vase on the table. Mama and Daddy's bedroom was at the end of the hallway. My room was off the sitting room. My bed had a warm quilt Mama made for me. Every time I walked into our home, I felt like I was getting a great big hug. But now that Daddy was gone, everything felt different.

One evening, Leonard and Olive Smith came for dinner. We didn't have much to serve them because Mama hadn't been to the corner store in weeks. I know she had a little money—I saw some in the pickle jar. Then a thought just came to me: maybe Mama didn't want to get back into Daddy's stubborn truck. Maybe she was too scared, or too hurt, or both to try again. I made up my mind right then and there I would learn to drive Daddy's truck. I watched Daddy enough, so I knew what to do.

Daddy always kept the keys in the truck, so now Mama did too. I would climb up in the truck, strain to push the clutch in, and turn the key, hoping it would not stall. Every time I would put it in gear, it would stall over and over again. I practiced every day for a week and was finally able to get it to move without stalling. I wore out the road in front of our house driving up one side and down the other. Mama watched me, but she didn't say much. I think she was hoping I'd learn and learn I did. From then on, I did the driving; I'd drive us to the grocery store and church every week.

The night Leonard and Olive came over, I came to realize that Mama's worries were bigger than just getting the fields planted. Leonard helped Mama "sort through her affairs," as he called it.

Mama kept saying, "I thought we had more than that."

I figured she was talking about money. Mama had never taken care of money; that was Daddy's job. It appeared we didn't have a whole lot of money to start with, and Daddy had spent the money we did have on a new tractor because his old tractor was wore out. He also spent a good bit on seed. Mama said Daddy gambled his money: he bet on having good crops this year. He was going to take care of his family by bringing in money from the fields. Trouble was, he wasn't here to work the fields.

Mama cried and cried after the Smith's left. She kept wringing her hands and saying out loud, "I don't know how we are going to make it."

"What's wrong Mama?" I asked. "What aren't we going to make?"

Mama looked at me for a moment. "This is my worry child. Don't you worry your young heart."

"But Mama, I'm not that young anymore. I'm old enough to drive you to the store and church," I reasoned.

Mama's resolve finally lifted, and she just let it all out, "Oh child, Daddy just didn't leave us much money. I just don't know what I'm supposed to do. I could sell the tractor, but Leonard said we would not be able to get what it's worth. Besides, we need the tractor to work the fields."

"Who is going to work the fields now that Daddy is gone?" I asked.

Mama looked at me, squared her shoulders, and said, "It will have to be you and me, child. I was going to hire help, but we just don't have the money to pay anybody."

"But Mama, you don't know anything about planting fields."

"I'm just going to have to learn, Evie. I'm just going to have to learn. Otherwise, we'll lose this farm Daddy worked so hard for."

Mama and I set out to plant the fields all by ourselves. We worked from sun-up to sun-down. If one of us couldn't lift something, we would help the other. We worked so hard. We worked until we were sore, and then we would crawl into bed. One morning, I was up before Mama. This never happened; Mama was always up at the crack of dawn. I went into Mama's room, and she was rising up out of bed.

She slowly stood up and said, "Land sakes! I didn't mean to sleep this long."

Mama had her thin nightdress on. For the first time, I noticed how skinny Mama had gotten. I guess I never paid attention before when she wore her normal dresses.

"Mama I can see your bones," I said to her with surprise in my voice.

She quickly grabbed her robe and put it on. "I suppose I need to start eating more," she said real quiet-like.

"Mama, I think you are working too hard in the fields."

"I have to keep going. It's the only way we are going to make it in this world."

She held her back and grimaced.

"Mama does your back hurt?" I asked, feeling sorry for her.

"Oh, I just need to walk it out some," she answered.

Mama went back in the field that day. I could tell by her face she was in a heap of pain. After the day's work was done, Mama said she was sure glad tomorrow was going to be Sunday. Mama and Daddy never believed in working the fields on the Lord's Day. She told me she would not be going to church. This was really rare for Mama. She said she needed to give her back time to heal.

"I want to stay home with you, Mama."

"No need both of us missing the Lord's message. Now you go on to church and come back and tell me what the message was about."

The next morning, I rose up to find Mama was true to her word. She was not going to church. She was sound asleep in bed. I didn't wake her. I had heard her up during the night. She *was* getting some of Daddy's pain pills out of the medicine box. I figured it must have been hurting pretty bad for her to

15

do that. I didn't wake Mama. I fixed myself some oatmeal and went on to church.

If truth be told, I really didn't like church. I only went because Mama wanted me to go. I liked it pretty good when Brother Martin preached the sermon, but Brother Martin was getting old and tended to repeat himself, so the church voted to bring in a new preacher.

Brother Al Jenkins was the new preacher's name. I didn't like him from the start. I wished that Brother Martin had preached at Daddy's funeral instead of Brother Jenkins. Everybody convinced Mama to have the new preacher do it because Brother Martin might just forget who the funeral was for. Mama was fearful he would forget right in the middle of it. It was said, he had done that before. Brother Martin might have been forgetful, but he wasn't fake. Brother Jenkins was fake through and through. Why the grown people in the church didn't see it, I didn't know.

After the service was over, everybody walked slowly out of the church. Brother Jenkins was standing at the door shaking everybody's hand with that fake smile on his face. I didn't want to shake his hand, but I didn't figure I had much of a choice.

He took hold of my hand tight and shook it.

"Where is your Mama?" he asked.

Evie

The only way I knew to answer him was honestly. "She hurt her back working in the fields. She is resting so it can be better come tomorrow morning."

"I am so sorry to hear that," he said with his fake voice that made me *burning* mad. "Tell her I would like to pay her a visit. I would like to pray for your dear mother and ask the Lord to take her pain away."

I didn't like Brother Jenkins one bit, but if he somehow had a way of praying that would make Mama better, I would be glad to have him come over.

"Yes, sir, I will tell her," I answered in the polite way Mama taught me, even though I didn't feel like being polite to him.

When I got home, Mama was sitting in Daddy's chair. I was glad to see she was up. I went over to Mama and gave her a careful hug.

"How are you feeling, Mama?"

"Better, child. How was the sermon?"

I felt bad—I could not remember one word of Brother Jenkins' sermon. I was daydreaming during the whole thing, but I didn't want Mama to know, so I fibbed a little and made up my own sermon.

As I rambled on, Mama must not have caught on because she kept shaking her head like she agreed with what I was saying. The made-up sermon was something I felt Mama needed to hear. I told her that God would take care of his children no matter what and we weren't to worry. If God cares about a little sparrow, well then, he surely cares about us. If I wasn't mistaken, my sermon made Mama's eye's mist over.

As I was walking out of the room, feeling a little ashamed about lying to Mama, I remembered Brother Jenkins telling me he would like to stop by.

Oh no! I thought guiltily. *I hope he doesn't talk about his sermon, because I'm sure his was nothing like mine.*

"Mama, Brother Jenkins said to tell you that he would like to stop by and pay you a visit. He would like to pray for you."

"Oh Evie, he mustn't come. I have nothing prepared for him," Mama said with a worrisome sound in her voice.

"Mama, he is not caring about that. He just wanted to pray for you."

"Oh, but Evie, you are not understanding. It is not proper to have a man of God in your home without offering him a meal," Mama explained fretfully. She looked at me with desperate eyes and asked, "Did he say when he was coming?"

"No, Mama, he didn't."

"Well then, we'll just need to figure on him coming for dinner," Mama stated flatly. "Here, help me up out of this chair so we can get some dinner cooking on the stove."

"Mama!" I complained.

"Don't argue with me, child! This is just the way it has to be."

Mama sat on the kitchen chair and started peeling potatoes while she instructed me on how to fry chicken. I figured the meal itself was more than enough, but Mama said we needed a dessert too. She said, "a man of God doesn't come for dinner without getting dessert as well."

So the day that was supposed to give Mama rest turned out to be a lot of worrisome work for her and for me.

Sure enough, Brother Jenkins showed up right at dinnertime. He knocked on the door and Mama invited him in. She had put on her best dress. She walked with a little limp. This told me her back still hurt

If Brother Jenkins was surprised we had dinner ready for him, he didn't act like it. He just came on in and handed me his suit coat. I didn't even offer to take it. He looked around the house and made comments like, "Nice house, good and sturdy." He acted more interested in the house than he did in Mama and me.

All through dinner all he talked about was himself. If Mama was annoyed by this, she didn't show it. She did have that fake smile on her face though. Brother Jenkins finished off a bunch of chicken, mashed potatoes, and green beans. When he helped himself to the chicken, I wondered if he didn't know that Mama and me would be eating too. He took nearly all Mama and me had cooked.

After dinner, we went into the sitting room for a spell. He talked more about himself, and then he said, "Ladies, you'll have to excuse me. I've got other house calls to make."

He headed for the door. "But Brother Jenkins, you haven't prayed for Mama."

He looked angry for a moment and mumbled something under his breath. Then he said, "Yes, of course. Let us pray."

He spilled out this prayer about how Jesus died on the cross and took our pain away. This all sounded right, but then he went on and on about things that didn't make sense. I just rolled my eyes at how fake he was.

Mama graciously said, "Thank you kindly, Brother Jenkins."

If I didn't know better, I would have thought Mama was blushing and batting her eyes. Surely Mama wasn't flirting with Brother Jenkins, was she? He said he would be back in a

Evie

few days to check on her. As he stepped off the porch steps, he looked around. He asked Mama how many acres our property had on it. I felt mad. This was not his business, but Mama answered him with a smile.

After Brother Jenkins left, Mama and I worked together washing the dishes. Mama gave me a look.

"Is anything wrong, Evie? You seem so quiet."

"I don't much like the new preacher, do you?"

"Oh, Evie, you should not judge him so. You don't even know him," Mama said in a strained voice.

I finished my dishes without answering. Maybe Mama was right: I needed to work on having a kinder heart like her.

Brother Jenkins came right back the next day. He told us God had spoken to him in the night. He said that God told him he was to help Mama and me with the farm. He went on to say that God told him other things he would reveal to Mama later, but now was not the time.

Mama seemed to be happy with what Brother Jenkins had said. She told Brother Jenkins he had just lifted a big burden off her shoulders. He touched Mama's shoulders and even rubbed them a little.

"Dear Laura, I would do anything to ease your burdens."

Mama blushed and smiled. It made me *burning* mad that he had touched her shoulder.

Brother Jenkins came over every day from then on. He said God told him to help us with the farm, but I noticed he got some men in the church to do it instead. He stood in front of the pulpit and announced to everybody that God had told him the men of the church were supposed to help the widows. He said the widow in need now was Laura Thompson and her daughter Evelyn. So, the men of the church, I'm sure fearing God's wrath, showed up one by one and helped Mama and me on the farm.

The farm never looked so good. Fields were tended to, fences were mended, and even the roof of both the barn and the house were replaced. Brother Jenkins did very little of the work. He spent most of his time with Mama. He seemed to never want me around. He found jobs for me to do outside my own house. This bothered me something fierce.

This one particular day I had had enough of Brother Jenkins bossing me around, so I yelled at him. "Brother Jenkins, I thought God told you to help Mama. Instead, you are acting like God told you to tell other people to help Mama."

He didn't like me saying that at all. He pierced his skinny lips together and made a "*hhmm*" sound.

"You're acting a little too big for your britches, young lady," he glared at me. "If you don't mind your manners, God will strike you down."

I never did like Brother Jenkins looks, but now I couldn't even stand looking at him. He had oily thin black hair. He had a long skinny body, which matched his long skinny mustache. He had small, black, beady eyes, which seemed to always be moving back and forth. How Mama could stand to sit there talking to him for hours was a mystery to me, but Mama wasn't really talking to him. She was listening to him.

Chapter 4

*O*ur lives went on like this for weeks. One day, Mama asked me to join her and Brother Al Jenkins in the sitting room. She said she had something important to talk to me about. What she had to say would change my life forever. Daddy's death had changed my life, but what Mama told me made sure my life would never ever be the same again.

"Evie, Brother Jenkins has asked for my hand in marriage, and I have accepted," Mama announced.

My mouth fell open. I looked from Mama to Brother Al Jenkins in disbelief. He stared back at me with triumph in his beady little eyes. Then he said something that made me want to kick him hard in the shin.

"Evelyn, I would be proud to take your Daddy's place and be your stepfather."

This did not set well with me. I could tell this didn't set well with Mama either because she said, "Oh, but Brother Al, I mean no disrespect, but no one could take her father's place."

Evie

"My dearest Laura, you are not even giving me the chance. I feel I could be a very good father."

"Yes, I'm sure you will, but you will not be able to take her father's place, as I said."

I was so proud of Mama for being firm on this matter.

"Let me make myself perfectly clear to both of you. When we marry, I will be Evie's father. I do not want her previous father, who is no longer on this earth, and is no worldly good to anyone, to even be mentioned."

I looked over at Mama, knowing full well she would break off this foolish engagement right then and there and kick him right out of our house.

Instead, she looked down, patted her eyes with the bottom of her apron, and said, "Yes, Brother Al."

I heard-tell what people feel like when they are getting ready to faint. I heard they get real lightheaded and the ground gets shaky.

Well, that's what happened to me.

Before I knew it, Brother Jenkins was behind me, dragging me to a chair. And Mama was saying my name over and over, "Evie-Evie, what is wrong child?"

After a while, I guess I came to. Mama brought me a glass of water. I took a few drinks, which made me feel better.

I just couldn't let my mind think on the things I had heard the last few minutes. I decided to pretend I didn't hear any of it.

Once I had convinced them I was all right, I asked to be excused. I went outside and just lay in the yard with Rusty, our big old Golden Retriever. Rusty must have realized I was going through something awful, because she licked me over and over. I think she was trying to tell me everything would be okay. But it wasn't okay. Nothing would ever be okay ever again.

Well, true to Mama's word, there was a wedding, and it happened only two weeks from the day I got the horrible news. I will say Mama did look pretty—except for the fake smile she had on her face. Come to think of it, I really hadn't seen Mama's real smile since before Daddy died. It was almost like the fake smile was becoming Mama's real smile. Mama's real smile died when Daddy died.

After Mama and Brother Jenkins were married, they went away for a few days. The day they came home, I noticed something different about Mama. I couldn't put my finger on it. She didn't seem sad or happy; she seemed numb.

"Mama, did you and Brother Jenkins enjoy your getaway?" I asked.

"Yes dear, we did," she answered. But I didn't believe her.

Evie

The men from church stopped coming over. Mama was no longer a widow and most of the work was done. Brother Jenkins did hire a farmhand to continue tending to the fields. He said his time was better spent doing God's work.

As the weeks went by, I noticed Mama looking even more pale and fragile. Brother Jenkins stayed away all during the day because he said he was tending to his flock. He would come home late at night, and he and Mama would go into the bedroom. One particular night, I could have sworn I heard her scream, then cry.

I knocked frantically on the door. "Mama, are you alright?"

"Yes, she is," Brother Jenkins answered.

But I knew she wasn't. I felt like Brother Jenkins was hurting Mama. I even noticed bruising on Mama's arms.

I flat out asked Mama, "Is Brother Jenkins hurting you, Mama?"

Mama paused for a long time, and then she looked at me with teary eyes and said, "Don't worry, sweetheart. I really don't want you to worry."

Chapter 5

As time went on, Mama finally admitted to me that Brother Jenkins wasn't the man she thought he was. It was on my fifteenth birthday. Mama had baked me my favorite chocolate cake. She was just putting the icing on it when Brother Jenkins stormed into the house, madder than a red hornet. He raved on and on.

What I could figure from his yelling is that Mama had gone into town a few days ago. She had visited with Doctor Hamilton. Doc had asked her about her bruises. Mama broke down in his office and confessed to him that Brother Jenkins was mistreating her. Doctor Hamilton promised not to say anything, but he had broken his promise and confronted Brother Jenkins about Mama's bruises.

Of course, Brother Jenkins had denied it. He said that Mama was a little touched in the head since Daddy's death. She had taken to hurting herself.

Brother Jenkins then told Mama that, because she betrayed him, he had no choice but to go around the whole town asking everyone to pray for his poor, unfortunate wife. He explained to everyone that he had married a woman who had gone crazy.

Mama looked at him in disbelief and shouted, "How could you do this to me?"

"It was easy," Brother Jenkins answered. "I can destroy you just as easy as I can destroy this cake."

He smashed his fist right through my chocolate cake. Mama screamed, grabbed my hand, and pulled me out the door. She and I ran into the safety of the barn.

We found a dark corner in the barn and huddled close together. I could feel Mama shake. I hugged her tighter.

Mama grabbed my face and said, "Evie, listen to me."

A little stream of light came through the barn window, revealing the desperation in Mama's eyes.

"Evie, I have made a terrible mistake by marrying Al Jenkins."

For the first time Mama didn't refer to him as Brother Jenkins.

"Oh Evie, I should have listened to you. You didn't want me to marry him, but I figured it was our only way. It's hard for a woman to get by in this world without a man. I wanted us to be safe, but we are not safe now. I fear we are great danger at the hands of this evil man."

Mama then took me by the shoulders and said, "Evie, our only way out of this horrible situation is to get away from him. He is an evil, intelligent man who is used to getting his way. I have a plan. I have to hurry and explain it to you before he comes out here looking for us."

Mama went on to tell me her plan. It was hard to understand her because she was crying, shivering, and talking fast all at the same time.

She explained that she had a cloth purse hidden in her dresser drawer. In this purse was a little money. It also contained a map to Grandpa's house, a deed to our land, Daddy's death certificate, a compass, and a letter. In the next few days, we were going to secretly pack our things, walk into town, get on a train, and travel to Grandpa's house. He lived in Trenton, Tennessee. I had not met Grandpa, but Mama talked about him a good bit. I felt I knew him from the things she had told me about him. Grandma died when Mama was a little girl, but Mama didn't talk about her much.

Before Mama and I had a chance to finish talking about our plan, we were startled by Al Jenkins coming out of the shadows of the barn and standing right in front of us, his hands on his waist. We were not sure what all he heard, but we were pretty sure he heard enough to make him crazy mad. He

Evie

grabbed Mama and yanked her hard, pulling her away from the barn and back into the house.

"You leave my Mama alone, Al Jenkins!" I shouted.

I had no more got those words out of my mouth when he was standing right in front of me. He pulled Mama back and slapped me hard in the face.

"Don't you refer to a man of God by calling him by name alone!" he screamed.

"You are not a man of God!" I screamed back. "A man of God is good man."

As I said those words, I looked into Mama's eyes. Her eyes were pleading with me to be quiet. I tried to pull Mama away, but Al Jenkins shoved me into the dirt.

Before he could hit me again, I stumbled to my feet and took off running down the road.

Chapter 6

I stayed gone a good long time. It was getting dark, so I decided to go home. The closer I got to home, the more uneasy I felt. I got the feeling of just knowing something was wrong. Something just wasn't right.

There was a strange quiet in the house when I opened the door. All the lights were off, except a little light in Mama's room. I slowly walked into Mama's room. She was lying on the bed. Her lip was swollen, and she was holding a rag on her head. She looked relieved when I walked over to her.

She sighed real big and touched my hair. I took hold of her hand, which felt weak.

"What happened to you Mama?"

"He hit me, and I fell and hit my head on the bed post," Mama explained in a faint whisper.

I caressed her hand between my fingers. My eyes fogged up with tears.

"Evie," she continued. "If something happens to me, I want you to go to your Grandpa's and stick to our plan. Make sure Al Jenkins is nowhere around. Then find the purse I told you about."

"Mama, what do you mean if something happens to you?" I shook my head in disbelief. "You don't mean die, do you? You ain't going to die Mama! Don't ever leave me Mama."

"Just remember what I said, Evie. Now go on to bed. God willing, I'll be better in the morning."

"Mama I don't want to leave you," I pleaded tearfully.

"Go, Evie. Go now," Mama pleaded. "I don't want Al to see you in here. I don't want him hitting on you."

So I left Mama's room. I tried to go to sleep, but I just tossed and turned all night. I finally fell asleep, but I woke up in the morning to the sound of men's voices. It was Al Jenkins and Doc Hamilton.

I ran out of the bedroom.

"What's wrong? Why are you here, Doc?" I asked.

"Go on back to bed," Al ordered roughly.

I ran past Al toward Mama's room, but Doc Hamilton caught me before I got in. "Evelyn, please come here."

I struggled out of his grasp, but he grabbed hold of me again.

"Evelyn, please! Listen to me."

"No!" I yelled, full of a panic that I couldn't explain. "I want to see Mama!"

"I have something to tell you," He explained. "Your mama died in her sleep. I am so sorry. Brother Jenkins said your Mama tripped and hit her head on the bedpost. This must have caused trauma to her brain, which caused her to stop breathing a few hours ago."

"No!" I screamed, "Mama can't be dead!"

I finally broke free from Doc Hamilton and ran into Mama's room.

She was lying still on the bed.

I fell on her chest and cried. "Mama wake up!"

She didn't move. She was cold and white.

"Please wake up," I pleaded.

But there was no answer.

I rose up from the bed, and a sense of knowing came over me. This was no longer Mama. Mama was now in heaven with Daddy. Mama died, and *he* killed her.

Suddenly, I felt rage.

"No!" I screamed. "Mama didn't trip and kill herself."

Both men had walked into the room. I pointed at Evil Al.

"He killed her! I talked to Mama last night and she told me Al Jenkins hit her hard in the head, knocking her against the bed post. Didn't you see the bruises on her face and the cut on her lip, Doc?" I cried "He killed her!"

I desperately wanted Doc Hamilton to believe me. But he just stared at me, mouth opening and closing, not saying a word.

Evil Al walked over to me with fake tears in his eyes. He got down on his knees and touched my face. I shuddered.

"Evie," he said. "I know you are as heartbroken as I am, but we both know your mother hasn't been, shall we say…" He paused "…hasn't been *right* since your daddy died."

He went on talking with fake compassion, all for Doc Hamilton's benefit.

"Evie, sweetheart, if it makes you feel better to blame me, go ahead. But I think your poor Mama wanted to hurt herself. I feel she wanted so badly to be with your daddy that, God rest her soul, she took her own life."

Doc Hamilton nodded his head like he believed everything Al Jenkins said. The men turned away from me like I wasn't in the room anymore. Doc told Al Jenkins he would be sending the undertaker over for Mama. He said he was sorry and asked if there was anyone he could call, or anything he could do.

Al Jenkins answered him in a fake sad voice, "No, thank you. Evelyn and I will take care of the funeral arrangements."

With a handshake and a nod, Doc Hamilton turned to leave. Before he went out the door, he glanced in my direction and shook his head to himself, like I was a pitiful, disrespectful child.

Well, I wasn't pitiful or disrespectful. Al Jenkins killed Mama and I knew if I hung around here long enough, he would kill me too.

Mama had told me if anything were to happen to her, I was to stick to our plan. I was to find her purse and go to Grandpa's house. I didn't have time to sit around and cry over Mama. I knew she would not want me to do that.

The undertakers came. They lifted Mama's body up and put her on the bed, a bed that you could carry. As they were moving her body out, I stopped them. I pulled back the sheets and took one last look at my sweet Mama's face. I bent down and whispered in her ear, "Bye, Mama. Say hi to Daddy. I love you and don't worry: I'll stick to our plan."

Later that day, Al Jenkins walked into my room. He looked at me with evil beady eyes and said, "I need to go into town and make funeral arrangements for your mother. I don't have time to deal with you now, but when I get back, I'm going to sit you down and give you some new rules. I'm in control now. You will do as I tell you. Am I making myself clear?"

My good sense told me if I didn't agree with this evil man, he would hit me, so I nodded my head in agreement.

"Ok good," Evil Al said. "Now give your step-dad a hug before I leave."

A hug! Never in my life would I give him a hug.

He came over to me and put his scrawny arms around me. Then he moved his hands across my chest and mumbled to himself, "Yes, they will do just fine."

He smiled, in that that evil way he did, and then left the house.

I ran to the window and watched him drive out of sight.

Now was my chance to escape.

Chapter 7

This is my chance! I thought. I need to go find Mama's purse and get away before Evil Al Jenkins gets back. Just thinking about him hugging me made my skin crawl.

I ran down the hall to Mama's room when I heard the sound of a car. My heart jumped in my chest. Had Evil Al come back already?

I hurried back to the window and saw Leonard and Opal Smith getting out of their truck. Opal was holding a cake.

It always puzzled me why people baked cakes for people when their kin folks died. Seemed to me that cakes are for celebrating. A funeral ain't no celebration. Mama and me had so much cake to eat after daddy died, I about got sick.

Leonard and Miss Opal tapped on the screen doors and then let themselves in.

"Evie," Miss Opal called into the house, "we came to pay our respects."

"Oh, thank you, Miss Opal," I said. She handed me what looked like a peanut butter cake. I sat the cake on the table, and before I could turn around Miss Opal had her arms around me.

"Oh, you poor, poor girl. First your Daddy, now your Mama. At least you have Brother Jenkins. I know he is not your daddy, but he is a man of God." Miss Opal went on rambling. "The Good Lord must have brought him to our town not only to be our preacher, but to be a daddy to you."

By this time, big tears were falling from Miss Opal's eyes. I wanted to scream that Al Jenkins would never be my Daddy. I wanted to scream that I hated him and that he killed my Mama, but the words wouldn't come out.

Instead, I just nodded my head in agreement. I figured if I started spouting off, I wouldn't be able to fulfill the plans Mama and me made. I figured the less I said, the sooner the Smiths would get on their way.

But Miss Opal didn't just bake the cake for me. Turned out she wanted some too. She insisted on cutting it before she left so we could all visit for a spell. Miss Opal had me put some water on for tea to go with the cake. After a while, it seemed like Miss Opal was stalling, she kept asking nosey questions about Al Jenkins. She smiled and smoothed her hair when she asked the questions. I think she was hoping he would walk in while she and Leonard were visiting.

Leonard was getting restless. He sighed and said, "Now Opal, if you are waiting to talk to the preacher we can stop back by later."

"Very well, Leonard, I just wanted to assure our dear Brother Jenkins that we are here if he ever needs anything, and I would be happy to lend a mother's touch to help our poor Evie if ever need be."

"Thank you, Miss Opal. I will remember that," I said politely.

That seemed to satisfy her.

"Alrighty then, we'll be on our way," Miss Opal said. She wrapped me in her plump arms and hugged me hard.

As soon as Miss Opal and Leonard left, I made my way to Mama's room.

It smelled just like her, like sweet spring flowers.

Being in Mama's room and smelling her sent caused me to miss her something awful. I felt like crawling into Mama's bed and crying, but crying would not bring her back. I had to keep moving. I had to carry out Mama's plan.

I looked through Mama's drawers. At first, I couldn't find it, but then I felt around the back of the drawer and there it was! I felt the soft leather purse.

I pulled it out of the drawer and emptied the contents on Mama's bed. All the items Mama had described were there, except she didn't mention that there was a letter in the purse for me. It was from Mama. She also had a letter for Grandpa.

Mama must have known there would be a chance she would not be coming with me to Grandpa's house.

I wanted to read the letter from Mama so bad, but I knew this was not the time. I had to hurry. I put all the items back in the purse except for the coin purse. I counted the money. Mama had saved seventy-eight dollars and thirty-five cents. She must have been saving for a long time.

Suddenly, I heard the door open.

A jolt of terror went down my spine.

Oh no! He's back!

I quick-like stuffed the purse in my dress pocket. I looked down and realized I forgot to put the money back in.

Evil Al was in the room before I could think twice. I put the money behind my back.

"What are you doing in here!" Al Jenkins yelled.

"I'm looking through my Mama's things," I stammered. "I miss her."

"These are not your Mama's things anymore! Everything in here belongs to me now!" He looked at me with those beady eyes. Suddenly, got suspicious. "What do you have behind your back, you little thief?"

I had to think fast. I held tight to the folded bills with one hand. With the other hand, I pulled out a few dollars. I was sure hoping I didn't pull away the twenty-dollar bill or one of the ten- dollar bills. Then I put the fisted hand with most of the money at my side, hidden in the folds of my dress.

I reached out my other hand to him, showing the few dollars I had.

"Mama said she was saving money for me, so I came to get it."

I was so relieved to see that I only had the five-dollar bill and two crumpled one-dollar bills in my hand.

"Give me that!" He grabbed the money from my hand and stuffed it into his pants pocket.

I held my breath, hoping he wouldn't notice my tight-fisted other hand. I'm glad Mama had the money folded up in tiny squares, otherwise I don't think I could have hidden.

I turned around to leave the room. As I did, I real secret-like stuck the money into my dress pocket.

Suddenly, I felt a big thud on the back of my head. It dazed me, and I fell against the doorframe for balance. I turned around and realized Al Jenkins had hit me hard. His fist was still clenched, ready for another blow.

"Let this be a lesson to you Missy," he snarled. Nothing in this house is yours, everything belongs to me! Even you!"

Evie

I knew I had to run, or I would end up dead at the hands of this man, just like Mama.

I ran to the front door.

Al Jenkins shouted after me, "Hey, where do you think you are going? You have a meal to cook for me!"

He caught up to me and grabbed my arm so tight I cried out. I had to do something fast, so I grabbed Mama's favorite lamp. I swung and hit him as hard as I could, square on the forehead.

Evil Al fell back, grabbing his skull and cursing. "You little bitch!"

Blood streamed down his face from the massive red bump on his scalp, but I hadn't knocked him out.

I opened the front door and ran out onto the porch. Evil Al ran after me and yanked a handful of my hair.

"Oww! Let go!" I screamed.

Suddenly, I noticed the Smith's pulling up into our yard. I was never so relieved to see anyone in my life. I felt the Lord must have sent them to save my life.

Leonard Smith jumped out of his truck and yelled, "What is going on here?"

I thought for sure Al Jenkins had been caught, but his mind worked fast.

43

"I'll tell you what's going on," he growled. "This little brat tried to kill me!"

I felt so much rage. I didn't want to hear one more lie from Al Jenkins.

I began spilling out everything. I told Leonard how Al Jenkins hit Mama, causing her to hit her head, which lead to her death, and how he said that everything that belonged to Mama belonged to him now.

"Shut up, you stupid girl!" Evil Al interrupted.

"You let her finish!" Leonard yelled.

I told him that I would be next that Al Jenkins wants me dead too.

Leonard set his jaw. "Get in the truck, Evie."

"Don't you dare, Evie," Evil Al snarled. "You stay right here!"

"Get in the truck!"

I got in the truck.

Leonard told Al Jenkins that he had known me and my family for a long time and he had never known any of us to lie. He went on to say that if he found out for sure that what Evie said was true, he would string Evil Al up by his testicles.

Leonard got in his truck. He looked madder than a hornet.

Evie

Miss Opal just kept wringing her hands and saying, "Oh my, I just can't believe all this."

The Smiths said I should stay with them until they could get to the bottom of why Brother Jenkins was acting so strange. Leonard said he would be speaking to some of the men in the church. I really wanted to get going with me and Mama's plans, but I figured one of Miss Opal's fine meals and a good night's sleep would do me some good.

Miss Opal informed me that Mama's funeral was going to be the day after tomorrow. She said considering the circumstances I would be going with her and Leonard to the funeral. Miss Opal didn't know it, but I planned on being well on my way to Grandpa's the day after tomorrow. Mama would want it this way. She knew I meant no disrespect by not showing up at her funeral.

Miss Opal fixed the sofa nice and comfortable for me. It looked like the Smiths had a second bedroom, but Miss Opal acted funny about it. She asked if I minded sleeping on the sofa, I said the sofa was fine. I was bone tired and the back of my head still hurt where Evil Al smacked me. Now whenever I think of Al Jenkins, I put the word "Evil" right in front of his name. It suits him real good.

It seemed I no more got to sleep when I heard a pounding on the door. I guess it was already morning, but it was sure early morning because it was still a bit dark outside. The Smiths were not even up out of bed.

Leonard stumbled to the door half-asleep, saying, "Who in tarnation is banging on the front door at this hour?"

He opened the front door and came face to face with Evil Al Jenkins and Sheriff Harrington.

"Morning, Leonard," the sheriff said. "I understand you have Evelyn Thompson here with you."

"Yes, I do," Leonard said. He pulled the sheriff aside to talk to him privately.

The sheriff held up his hand and said, "No need to explain, Leonard. Brother Jenkins told me everything."

Evil Al was standing in the room, letting the sheriff do all the talking with that sly, evil look on his face. He glared at me. I was glad to see the goose egg I gave him was still on his forehead.

The sheriff spoke up again, "Yeah, Brother Jenkins has dealt with these matters before, him being in God's service and all. He told me that Evie just can't cope with her Mama killing herself, so she is blaming him. Because he is the man he is, he said she could blame him if she needs to—anything to help Evie cope with her loss. Personally, I think she is just a young girl acting up. Never-the-less, Leonard, Brother Jenkins has custody of the girl now."

Everything the sheriff was saying made me steaming mad. Didn't he realize what a big evil liar Evil Al is?

"Well now, sheriff, I don't think I feel right just handing her back over to Jenkins. As I said, he was roughing her up pretty good on her front porch yesterday."

Just as Leonard said those words, Miss Opal put her arms around me in a real protective kind of way. "Don't worry, child, she whispered."

"Well, Leonard," the sheriff said, "I think Brother Jenkins was just laying down the law. He was exerting his parental rights by showing the girl a firm hand."

"But sheriff," Leonard pleaded.

"Sorry, Leonard. I'd have to arrest you if you didn't let Evie go back to her stepdad. He has legal right to her, not you."

Leonard walked over to me and whispered, "Evie, I'm sorry you'll have to go with him now. I believe what you told me. We'll just have to figure a way to get you away from him, that's all."

"No, Leonard! We can't let her go with him," Miss Opal pleaded, holding on to me tight.

"Hmmph," Evil Al grunted. "My time is valuable. I have God's work to attend to. I would like to stay and continue our visit, but we must be on our way. Come along, Evie."

"No!" I screamed.

"Do you want the Smiths to be arrested?" the sheriff asked me, talking to me more like I was five years old instead of fifteen.

"No," I answered.

"Then I suggest you make up your mind and be obedient and mind your step-father."

I didn't want the Smiths to get arrested, so I had no choice, I had to go with Evil Al. I promised myself I would get away from him the first chance I got.

I hugged Leonard and Miss Opal, telling them not to worry, that I would be fine. Both Leonard and Miss Opal had tears in their eyes. Evil Al and me rode home without saying a word.

Evil Al didn't kill me that night. I guess he figured it would look too suspicious if I turned up dead right away. He made me cook him dinner. He told me if I didn't, he would wear me out real good because that is what good dads did when their children didn't behave. He told me I was his kid and I had to do as he said.

Evie

After dinner, Evil Al went outside. I peeked out the window to see what he was doing. He was smoking a pipe. I remember a sermon he preached talking about the evils of tobacco and liquor, and there he was smoking. I wasn't a bit surprised.

I thought about sneaking out of the other side of the house and getting on with Mama's plan, but then I changed my mind. I figured since he was outside too, he was liable to catch me. No telling what he would do to me, but what would he do to me when he came back in the house? Mama kept a hammer under the kitchen sink— "for safe keeping," she would always say. I knew it was to protect us from prowlers. Of course, we never had to use it, but it gave us comfort, especially when daddy was away. I got the hammer and stuck it under my pillow just in case I needed it.

I stayed in my room with my door closed all evening. I laid in bed thinking on the "get away" plan. I wondered, did Mama mean for us to walk to Grandpa's or take a train? It seemed like a mighty long way to walk. I wanted to take the map out and study it, but I didn't want to take the chance of Evil Al finding it, so I kept it safe in my dress pocket. I would just have to sleep in my dress.

I fell asleep, and the next thing I knew Evil Al was lying beside me. It scared me to death to see him lying there. I had to tell myself to breath.

"Evelyn, sweetheart. Don't be frightened. I just want to make up for all the pain I have caused you. You have a choice: you can either accept my apology or meet up with your Mama and Daddy in heaven and, by the way," Evil Al said with an evil smirk on his face, "Dimwit Leonard and his fat wife will be joining them soon."

"What are you going to do to me?" I whispered in panic.

"Don't worry. You'll love what I do to you."

He put his ugly lips over mine and forced his wet stinking tongue in my mouth. I couldn't help it; I threw up in his mouth.

He spit over and over, screaming, "Yuk! You sickening little tramp! Get ready to see your Mama and Daddy. I'll tell everyone it was self-defense from a crazed orphan."

He raised his hand to hit me, but I was quicker. I grabbed the hammer out from under my pillow and cracked him right on top of his head. He yelled, "You little bit…" But before he could get the word out, he fell limp and passed out. It took all my strength, but I slid out from under him, stood up, and hit him again on the back of the head just to make sure he

Evie

didn't move anytime soon. Maybe he would never move again, if I were lucky. I made sure Mama's purse was still deep in my pocket and took off running as fast as I could.

I had to run to Leonard and Miss Opal's house first to warn them about Evil Al's plan to kill them. Running to the Smiths reminded me of running there after daddy died. I was running for Daddy's life then, but now I was running for the Smith's life and my own.

I'm a year older now my legs are moving a little faster than they did a year ago. I need to be careful though: back then it was daylight, now it's pitch dark.

I banged on the door urgently. *Pound-Pound-Pound.*

Come on, Leonard! Open the door! I need to warn ya'll before he comes to and decides to come after me.

Still no answer. I decided to try the knob, and to my surprise the door opened.

"Leonard! Miss Opal!" I yelled.

They didn't answer me. Their house sure smelled something awful. I covered my nose and mouth with my hand. It smelled like when the pilot light went out on Mama's stove. I walked over to the Smiths' stove. Dadgum. Every single burner was on. I quickly turned them off, remembering that Daddy said it was very dangerous to smell gas too long. I ran and opened the front and back door and several windows. Then I ran into the Smiths' bedroom.

I almost tripped on Skipper, their dog. He was lying in the doorway.

"Skipper, wake up!" I shouted.

He couldn't wake up. He was as dead as a door nail. I ran to see about Leonard and Miss Opal.

"Leonard, you and Miss Opal need to get up! Your stove burners were left on! There's gas in the house!"

Oh no! Leonard and Miss Opal are dead too! I realized.

Suddenly, I heard a car pull up. Then I remembered I had opened the front door. I ran to close it and saw lights shining through the windows.

Oh no! It looks like it could be Daddy's truck. Evil Al must have come too! He'll kill me for sure!

I ran as fast as I could out the back door and across the yard. I jumped behind the shed. My heart was pounding so hard I thought it was going to pound right out of my chest.

I hid behind the shed for what seemed like hours, but it was only minutes. I didn't dare move a muscle. Suddenly, I saw him. He walked out the back door carrying a lantern. There was a fence behind the shed. I needed to crawl over to it.

Evie

This would put me into the field and woods behind the Smith's house. Then I would be able to run away. I saw him coming towards the shed! It was now or never.

I threw myself up over the fence, but the fence was so high I fell back down!

Darn it!

Leonard must have built the fence high to keep the coyotes out of his yard.

Evil Al was getting closer.

I tried again with everything I had in me. I knew this jump was a matter of life or death. I made it! I also made a loud thud noise which made Evil Al know exactly where I was. I knew I had to get away, and fast. I ran into the field and just kept running through the field and into the woods.

I heard Evil Al yell something, but I couldn't make out what. I kept running and running I ran in a zig-zag way, just in case he would try to follow me. I didn't want him to know which direction I was going. Daddy said this was what deer and rabbits did when they felt in danger. Well, tonight I had turned into a deer. The sky was extra dark because the moon was just a sliver. I sure was thankful for that.

I laughed to myself. *I bet Evil Al isn't following me. He is too much of a coward to run into the darkness, especially into the woods. He is an evil, crazy coward.*

My mind was racing. As I ran in the woods, I wondered if Evil Al had left and convinced the sheriff to come after me. My legs were feeling wobbly. I just couldn't go any farther. I fell down on a grassy area and went to sleep.

Chapter 8

I woke up with the sun shining on my face. I was on the edge of a field. I could see a farmhouse on the other side of the field. I had no idea where I was. I sat up, rubbed my eyes, and thought about everything that had happened the last couple of days. I guess Evil Al had done the Smiths in, just like he did Mama and was about to do to me. Why God didn't put an end to his evil ways by causing death upon him, I don't know.

"Dear Lord," I prayed, "please don't allow anyone else to die at the hands of Evil Al."

I had to keep moving, I wondered which way I should go. I remembered Mama's compass. I reached in my pocket to take out Mama's purse.

Oh no! The purse wasn't there!

I felt in the other pocket, but it wasn't there either. I looked on the ground, thinking maybe it had fallen out while I slept. I retraced my steps and looked all over. Mama's purse was nowhere to be found. Then I realized the purse must have fallen out when I jumped over the fence!

I had to go back and find the purse. How else would I know how to get to Grandpa Owens' house? I need the money Mama saved for me to help me get there. I just had to turn back, that was all there was to it. Mama used to say, "When things get hard, just pray to the Good Lord. He will give you the strength you need to see you through."

So that's what I was going to do.

"Dear Lord, as you probably know my life has been real hard since Daddy died. I've hit on some bad luck. I really need my luck to turn around, so if you can see fit, please help me get to Grandpa Owens' house. I'll need to find Mama's purse to help me get there. Thank you, Good Lord, for your help. Amen. Oh, and also Lord could you protect me from getting killed by Evil Al, and could you stop him from killing other people? Amen."

I took a few good breaths and started back the way I came. Suddenly, I felt "a rumble" coming from my stomach. I could never remember being so hungry. I realized I needed to eat or else I wouldn't be able to walk very far. I figured I could try to walk over to the nearby farmhouse. I thought maybe the people who lived there would be kind and give me a biscuit and water. If I weren't so hungry, I might have been too scared to go up to some stranger's house and ask for a biscuit, but I knew I needed to eat.

Evie

I walked through the field and had just got to the barn when a sound startled me.

Woof! Woof!

Dogs!

I ran into the barn and up into the hay loft, my heart racing. Then I heard voices.

"Hey Goldie, stop yer yelpin!" I heard a deep voice say.

"It must have been a squirrel or a rabbit" another man said.

My heart was pounding so loud I was afraid the men would hear it. I waited a while until I didn't see or hear the men anymore. They must have left, and the dogs went with them.

I had noticed when I stepped into the barn earlier that there was some horse feed. Horse feed ain't biscuits, but at least it was something. If it wouldn't kill a horse, it wouldn't kill me, I reckoned. I stuffed a bunch into my dress pocket, which reminded me of Mama's missing purse.

Lord, I sure hope I find that purse.

I noticed a bowl of water in the barn. I figured it was for the dogs. It looked to have a little dirt settled on the bottom, but I was thirsty so I drank it anyway. I figured a little dirt never hurt anybody. Dirt or not, it sure tasted good. I drank the whole bowl-full.

I slowly walked out of the barn. Luckily, there was no one in sight. I spotted a chicken coop. I walked inside and noticed five eggs laying there in plain sight. I was so hungry I didn't even hesitate: I grabbed one of the eggs and broke it. I raised it to my mouth to eat, but the whole slimy mess fell to the ground.

I stared at the wasted egg spilled on the grass. I had to figure out a way to eat it. I found a sharp stick and used it to poke a little hole in the shell. Then I tipped my head back and let the slimy nourishment run down my throat. Trouble was, as soon as the egg went down my throat, I thought of Evil Al sticking his rotten tongue in my mouth.

I threw it all up.

Wiping my mouth of egg, I realized that if I wanted the hunger pains to go away, I needed to try it again. I poked another egg and thought of how Mama would tell me how good eggs were for me. She would say they were full of protein and would make me strong. Mama's fried eggs were a heap better than these slimy things. The third egg I tried to eat finally went down my throat.

As I was getting ready to walk across the field again, I heard the squealing sound of pigs. I walked to the other side of the barn and, sure enough, there were three pigs in a pin. It looked as if a slop bucket had been emptied out into the pig pen, and what do you know, there were two whole biscuits just waiting for me to reach in and get them.

    I grabbed them. They were a little wet but still 'fitten to eat. The pigs didn't even holler. It was almost like they were expecting me. Maybe this was a sign things were getting better for me.

Chapter 9

I stuffed the biscuits in my pocket with the horse feed and took off running across the field back into the woods. I ran for several miles. Then I slowed down and starting walking. I figured there was no need to hurry. I wasn't being chased anymore—at least I sure hoped not. I would be so relieved to find the purse and continue on with me and Mama's plan, that's for sure.

After running and walking a good long while, my feet started to hurt something fierce. I felt I had one hundred needles poking in them. I sat down on a fallen tree to rest and look at my feet. I had on the leather flats Mama had bought me to wear to Daddy's funeral. It was a good thing my feet didn't grow any after that. Mama didn't have the money to buy me another pair of shoes. I guess I just wore the soles clean down because they weren't doing my feet any good anymore.

When I took my shoes off, I noticed I had blisters all over them. I remembered I wasn't too far from the creek. My blistered feet sure would feel better if I could put them in cold water. I couldn't put my shoes back on without putting

Evie

something between my blisters and my shoes, so I tore the hem right off my dress. I tore little pieces off with my teeth and made myself bandages. I put a bandage on each heel and on each side of my toes. It was hard to put my shoes back on, but I know I had to so I could make it to the creek.

The creek was farther away than I thought it would be. Finally, after walking quite a distance, I noticed the glistening of the water. I was sure happy to see the water. My feet were especially happy. I sat right down at the edge of the creek. My "worn out" flats were sure hard to get off. I guess my feet had swelled up some. The bandages I made were soaked plum full of blood. I put my bloody feet in the water and yelped in pain. They burned like the dickens!

I took my feet out for a minute and put them back in. They still stung something fierce, but soon the cool creek water made them feel a whole lot better.

I cupped my hands to give myself water. I was sure thirsty. I drank and drank. After many handfuls, I finally felt like I had my fill. I sure was feeling tired again. Before I knew it, I curled right up in a ball and went to sleep alongside the creek. I woke up feeling rain hitting me hard in the face. I saw sparks of lightning in the sky and heard crackle of thunder all around. I sure didn't want to get struck by lightning, so I found a wide, short bush to crawl under. I waited out the storm.

Somehow, I felt safer crouched under the bush than I had felt in a long time.

The storm had passed but I still heard rumbling. It was the sound of my hungry belly. I reached for the biscuits: they were now all crumbled up and mixed together with the deer feed. I grabbed the mushy mess, shaped it into little balls, and plopped one in my mouth. It tasted like sour milk and wood, but at least it was something to put in my belly. I forced myself to eat a little more. I limped over to the stream and drank some more water.

I tried to put my shoes back on, but my feet were too swollen and sore. I would just have to walk barefoot, that's all. It wouldn't be easy walking barefoot through the woods, but I would have to do the best I could.

Everywhere I walked, I looked for Mama's purse. I did fall a few times while running through the woods. Hopefully, it fell out during one of my falls and not when I jumped over the fence.

If I did lose it when I jumped over the fence, I pray Evil Al didn't find it.

If Evil Al had the purse, me and Mama's plan would be ruined. The thought brought tears to my eyes.

Evie

Dear Lord, help me find Mama's purse, I prayed out loud. I don't have any other plan except the one me and Mama made.

No use wasting time here at the creek. I needed to find the purse, get the compass and map, and find my way to Grandpa's house. I walked for several more miles. Finally, I saw the roof of the Smiths' house. It was a relief to see a familiar sight, but it also made my heart sad. They were dear friends to Mama and me, and sadly, they were dead too.

I walked slowly up to the fence with my heart in my throat, hoping beyond all hope that the purse was there. I searched the entire area where I thought I had jumped, but I could not find the purse.

Oh no! Panic swelled up within me.

How would I find Grandpa's house now? I sat right there on the ground. I could not help myself—I began to cry. I felt so hopeless. I just didn't know what to do without the purse. Through my tears, I noticed something shiny a few feet away. I got up and ran to the object and brushed away the leaves. It was Mama's compass!

But where was Mama's purse and all the things that were in it? Just as I thought those thoughts, I looked near the fence and there and the base of the fence was the purse. I guess I had been wrong about where I had jumped over the fence. It had been dark and I didn't realize exactly where I was. I grabbed the purse and frantically checked to see if the money, the letters, the map, everything was all still there.

The best I could figure was that the compass fell out because it was the heaviest thing in the purse. I also couldn't help but think Mama had sent me a sign to help me know that she was with me and I should continue on with our plan. As I thought of Mama, I remembered the letter she had put in the purse for me. I guess this was as good a time as any to read it. I was real curious about what it said. I just never had time to read it while running away from Evil Al.

I figured I could take a little time now. I leaned up next to the fence so no one would see me. I reached back in the purse and found the letter, along with the paper that looked to be a birth certificate. It seemed to be mine, only it was a bit confusing: it had my birth date and my first name, but it wasn't my correct last name; it was Mama's maiden name. I began to read the letter:

> *My Dear Sweet Evie,*
> *If you are reading this letter it means something has happened to me.*

Evie

I want you to know I love you so much. You are a very special girl. Your Daddy and I have always been so proud of you.

You need to get to Grandpa's house. Grandpa will make sure you are safe.

Evie, there is something else I need to tell you. This will come as a shock to you. I wish I would have told you in person. But since I am not there, I pray the good Lord will give you comfort when you read what I'm about to tell you. If you have looked at your birth certificate, you have noticed your last name is different than your Daddy's and mine. Your legal name is actually Owens. Owens, as you know, is my "maiden" name. You have my "maiden" name because we are sisters.

My mouth fell open in shock. I stared at the last line: "we are sisters."

What was Mama talking about? I kept reading.

You and I have the same biological father. I took you to raise as my own because our

65

mother had you late in life and died giving birth to you.

Daddy couldn't cope with losing Mother and taking care of a newborn baby. Your Daddy and I could not have children of our own, so taking you and raising you was a blessing for us.

Tears welled up in my eyes. My mind raced as I tried to understand.

You deserve to know the truth. I don't know if you would have received the truth any other way but for me telling you.

I have written my Daddy—our Daddy—about you. I told him what a lovely-young-women you have become. I know he loves you and will be able to take care of you, now that you are no longer a child. Please be a brave girl. I know what I have told you must come as quite a shock. Please forgive me for not telling you earlier in your life. Forgive me for dying and not being able to take care of you myself. Evie, trust the Lord to guide you and take care of you. I am putting you in his care as I struggle to write this letter.

With Love Always,
   Mother

    I read it through three times. Each time I read it, I wondered the same thing. How could Mama and Daddy not be my real Mama and Daddy? Mama was my sister, so that meant Daddy was no blood kin to me at all.

    I laid in the grass by the fence and cried and cried

    After I cried all the tears I could, I felt a peaceful feeling come over me. Mama asked me to be brave, so that's exactly what I was going to be. I didn't care if she was my sister; she was Mama and that's the way she would stay in my mind and in my heart. Daddy was going to stay Daddy, and Grandpa was going to stay Grandpa.

Chapter 10

As I sat near the fence wondering what my next move should be, I looked down at my feet and noticed they were bleeding something awful. If I didn't doctor them soon, I wouldn't be able to walk on them at all. I decided to be brave and go back to Opal and Leonard's house, hoping I could find something to mend my feet. I prayed that there was no one in the house—including their dead bodies. I shuddered to think of finding them like I found Skipper.

In my heart, I know Leonard and Miss Opal would not think me stealing if I took something from their house. They would want me to get whatever I needed to help me on my journey to Grandpa's. So, I jumped over the fence again, careful not to drop the purse.

I carefully walked through the backyard up to the back door. I put my ear against the door and listened for any sounds from inside. I couldn't hear anything, so I turned the doorknob and, luckily, the door opened. The house smelled musty. I walked into Leonard and Opal's bedroom with dread,

Evie

squinting my eyes so that I could close them if they were in there. The room was empty. I breathed a heavy sigh of relief. I was sure thankful they weren't still laying there.

It had been over a day since I had been here. Someone must have found them. Their bodies were probably up at Wilson's funeral home getting ready to be buried. I wondered when the funeral would be. I sure wished I could go. I knew Leonard and Opal are in heaven with Mama and Daddy 'cause they were real good people. They were probably up there praying to help me get out of this terrible fix I'm in.

My dress was soaking wet from the storm. I really needed to take it off and let it dry. I sure wished Miss Opal would not have been so daggum big cause then I could wear something of hers. What I really need are some britches. This dress was mighty cumbersome to be traveling in.

I noticed an apple pie on the table on the back porch. Miss Opal must have left it there to cool off. It was outside and covered, so I was sure it was okay and hadn't been spoiled by the gas fumes. I got myself a plate and cut a big slice of pie and poured myself a glass of sweet milk. I don't figure the Smiths would mind. They wouldn't want it to go to waste. The pie sure tasted good after eating them mushy horse feed balls.

I figured I'd better hurry and dry my dress and doctor my foot before someone took a notion to come to the Smiths' house. I took my dress off and laid it on a chair to dry. I kept my undergarments on and went out back to get some water from the well. Then I got to mending my feet. I found some salve and bandages and put them on my blisters.

I began looking around the house, hoping to find a pair of shoes that would fit. Maybe Miss Opal's feet were not big like her body was. I found a pair of her shoes in the corner of the room. I could tell by looking at them they would not fit. My hunch was right: they were about three sizes too big. I was disappointed. I would have to make my shoes work somehow. I couldn't travel the country with no shoes. Hopefully, I could stay here long enough for my feet to heal.

I continued to search the house for anything that would help me on my journey. I opened the door to a closed room. Miss Opal had acted funny about this room when I stayed with them. The room looked like it once belonged to a child. A young boy. I remember Mama using her proper voice saying that Leonard and Miss Opal had experienced a great sadness at one time in their life.

As I looked around the room, I noticed a ball and bat in the corner, along with a baseball cap hanging on a nail. There were story books stacked on the desk. In the other corner of the room were a pair of black shinny shoes and a pair of small work boots. Against the wall was a dresser. I opened the top drawer. In the drawer were three pairs of boy's underwear and two pairs of socks. In the second drawer were two white dress shirts and grey trousers. In the third drawer were two pairs of blue jeans. One pair was worn thin with patches on the knee. The other looked to be almost new. There were also two shirts. One shirt was thin cotton and the other was thick flannel. As I looked at the clothes, a thought came to me.

The clothes look like they would fit me. I could travel to Grandpa's disguised as a boy.

I took off my underthings and stood buck naked in the Smith's house. I opened the top drawer, grabbed the boy's underwear, and put them on. Then I put on the thin plaid shirt and new pair of blue jeans. It all fit. I took the cotton socks and real careful-like put them on my feet. I grabbed the boots and said a prayer that they would also fit. Sure enough, they fit me too, which I was mighty relieved about. I suddenly felt very thankful to the young boy these clothes had belonged to.

I opened the last drawer out of curiosity and found a big envelope in the drawer. Figuring it didn't really matter if I was nosy, I went ahead and opened it. Mama would have had my hide if she knew I went plundering through drawers, but Mama wasn't here.

I opened the envelope, which contained a birth certificate and a death certificate. The death certificate said that

Cody Leonard Smith died of pneumonia at age twelve. As I looked around the room, I realized everything was as it was when Cody was alive. Miss Opal probably could not bear to move her little boy's things from his room. Suddenly. I felt very grateful to Cody. I felt God supplied the things I needed through this boy.

I bowed my head and prayed, "Dear Lord, and Cody, thank you for the use of your clothes and boots. I hope you don't mind me wearing them."

I felt joyful imagining Miss Opal and Leonard seeing and hugging their son again. They must be very happy and rejoicing right now.

Suddenly, I heard a door open. There were voices. I quickly grabbed my underwear and crawled under Cody's bed.

"See, I told you she must have done it. Here's her dress."

Why did I leave my dress in the chair? I should have been more careful!

"But Brother Jenkins, what cause would she have to kill the very people who helped her?" the sheriff asked.

Oh no! Evil Al is trying to blame me for the Smith's death.

I had to hold myself down to keep from jumping out and screaming at Evil Al for being such a liar. I was in a heap of trouble now, but things would get a whole lot worse. I kept still under the bed, waiting for them to leave, but I was madder than a red hornet.

I was relieved to hear that the sheriff wasn't quick to blame me.

"It's suspicious that she left town," the sheriff said, "but I don't have proof that she killed the Smiths. It's possible that they died accidentally by leaving the gas on." He paused. "You sure are quick to accuse that step-daughter of yours."

"She's a very troubled young lady," Evil Al said in that smooth voice of his.

"Well, as soon as we find her, we'll question her real good," the sheriff said firmly.

No, they won't question me, I thought, *cause I'm going to be clean out of town before they find me! They ain't putting me in jail for something I didn't do.*

After a few more minutes, the two men left. I knew I didn't have much time before someone else came to the Smiths'. I needed to gather supplies. I looked around the house for something to put food in. I grabbed one of Miss Opal's aprons and filled it with two apples, crackers, cheese and some raisins. I bundled it all up and tied the strings of the apron around it for easy carrying.

I went into Miss Opal's and Leonard's room. There was still a smell of death there. I said a silent prayer for my dear friends, hoping they would get the funeral they deserved.

Miss Opal had a standing mirror in the corner of the bedroom. I studied myself real good. I had Mama's light brown hair. It curled a little, but not as much a Mama's. It was already getting real long past my shoulders. Mama always kept it trimmed up, but ever since she took up with Evil Al, it hadn't been cut. My face looked a lot like Mama's too. When people at church said we favored each other, I felt real good about that cause I always thought Mama was real pretty. Thinking of Mama made my eyes fill up with tears, but for Mama's sake I had to stay strong.

I figured the best way to get through this town without being recognized was to make myself look as much like a boy as I could. I'd probably be a little safer traveling the country as a boy too. My chest area had grown some here lately, which would give me away as being a girl for sure. I needed to bind myself up somehow. I took off the thin flannel shirt and stood there naked in front of the mirror. Sometime in these last few months I had started looking more like a "grown woman."

I looked around the room for something to tie around my chest. Miss Opal had a scarf on her chest of drawers. I tied it around my chest real tight. I put the shirt back on. The scarf worked: I looked as flat as a boy now. The problem was my hair didn't look like a boy. I figured the best thing to do was cut it all off. I found a pair of scissors in Miss Opal's sewing box. I started cutting big chunks of hair off. When I got done, I looked like a boy with a horrible haircut. I remembered the baseball cap in the boy's room. I got it and plopped it on my head. My face still looked a bit girlie, so I reached into Miss Opal's potted violet, got some dirt, and smeared it on my face. I didn't so much look like a girl anymore, just a real pitiful-looking boy.

    I quick-like grabbed my bundle of food. I figured I'd better put more salve and bandages in the pouch. I would probably need to doctor my feet later. They were still so darn sore.

    I stuffed all the things from Mama's purse into my pockets. I put the letters, money, and map in my pants pocket. I put the compass in my shirt pocket. I couldn't part with Mama's purse, so I rolled up the soft leather purse and put it in the pouch.

    My hair was all over Miss Opal's bedroom floor. I found a broom, swept up the hair, and buried it deep in the trash can. Just as I was throwing the last of my hair away, I heard a car door open. I looked out the window.

    Oh no! It was Evil Al getting out of Daddy's truck!

I didn't have time to get out the door, so I grabbed the apron filled with all my belongings and quick-scooted under Opal and Leonard's bed. I heard Evil Al walk in the door and wondered what he was doing coming back to the Smith's house. His footsteps got closer—he walked into the bedroom! My heart was pounding so hard it was thumping on the wood floor. Very carefully, mindful to stay quiet, I propped myself up on my forearms so my loud heartbeat wouldn't give me away.

I saw Evil Al's feet. He was so close!

I held my breath.

He walked over to chest of drawers. I scooted to the edge of the bed so I could see what he was doing, careful not to let him see me. He opened Miss Opal's jewelry box and, calm as you like, put her jewelry in his pocket. Evil Al was stealing from Miss Opal! I saw him take something else out of the drawer. I couldn't tell what it was, but he put that in his pocket too. Evil Al was a murderer, a liar, *and* a thief. I felt like getting out from under the bed and kicking him hard and make him put all everything back.

I wanted to get Daddy's truck back too. Evil Al had no right to Daddy's truck.

That's when the idea struck me: I would take back what was mine.

Daddy sure wouldn't want Evil Al driving around in his truck. He would want me to have it. But how would I get it? I would have to think quick.

Evil Al left the room. He was headed towards Cody's room. He wouldn't be in there long, 'cause there wasn't anything valuable in there. I didn't want to waste my chance. I scooted out from under the bed, making sure I had the pouch, and ran as fast as I could out the front door and right into Daddy's truck.

Thank goodness Evil Al had left the keys in the ignition. I turned the key.

The truck sputtered but didn't start.

The rumble of the truck engine brought Evil Al running out the door.

"Hey! You damn kid! Get out of my car, you little thief!"

I pleaded for the truck start. *Dear Lord, please let Daddy's truck start.*

I no more got those words out than the engine fired right up. Before I could take off, Evil Al wrenched the door open. He put his hand on my arm but I stepped on the gas and held on the steering wheel for dear life.

It was just in time: Evil Al let go of my hand and lost his footing. I saw him stumbled into the dirt from the rearview mirror.

He ran after me, yelling, "Come back here, boy! Thief! Thief!"

But I was long gone, driving away as fast as I could. I couldn't help but grin from ear to ear just thinking about the look on Evil Al's face. He hadn't recognized me either. I felt so thankful I could drive to Grandpa's house rather than walk.

Chapter 11

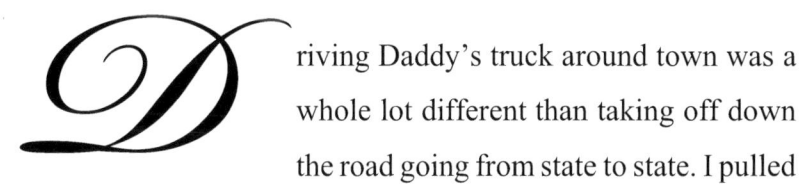

Driving Daddy's truck around town was a whole lot different than taking off down the road going from state to state. I pulled off to the side of the road to get the map and compass out of my pocket and see which way I was supposed to be going.

I sure hope I didn't look too suspicious being that I was just fourteen driving around in a truck. I looked like some young boy that wasn't big enough to be driving around. I hope people just figured I was small for my age. In a few months, I will be fifteen.

Thinking of my birthday made me realize I would sure miss Mama. She always baked me the best chocolate cake you ever did sink your teeth into. It made my mouth water just thinking about it.

As I looked at the map, I could tell Mama tried to make it easy for me to understand. But it was still confusing.

Lord, please help me find my way to Grandpa's house.

As I prayed that prayer, I remembered the letter Mama wrote me, letting me know that Grandpa was my real daddy.

My mind spun at the thought, I couldn't think about that right now. I had to put it away. I would come back to it at another time, when I had more time to think on it. Right now, I had to put all my thoughts into getting to Grandpa's house.

As I looked over the map, it looked like I was headed in the wrong direction. I would have to turn around and go the other direction. This meant I would have to go back through town. I didn't want to, but I didn't have a choice. I sure couldn't run the risk of being seen. I figured the best thing to do was to pull off the road and wait until dark. I knew Evil Al had already told the sheriff that somebody took off with his truck.

I decided to drive to a hidden spot where I wouldn't be seen. I drove to a little country road. While I sat waiting for nightfall, I nibbled on cheese and crackers. As I ate, I continued to study the map. I tried to figure out how long it would take to get to Grandpa's house.

I sure hope Grandpa doesn't mind me living with him, at least for a time.

As I waited for nightfall, I sure felt lonely. Mama always told me that living people were not supposed to have conversations with the dead. We were only to pray and talk to the Lord, but I couldn't help it: I just needed to talk to Daddy.

Evie

I sat there and told Daddy how I missed him, and how I sure wished he wouldn't have died.

"I know it wasn't your fault that you had a heart attack and fell off the tractor, but to tell you the truth, things got pretty rotten after you left. Things just haven't felt right at all. I guess you and Mama have met up by now. I'm sure she left out telling you all the bad stuff that has happened to us, so I won't burden you either. I sure am glad you and Mama are together."

I got so caught up talking to Daddy I didn't realize it was already dark. I pulled out of the country road. I drove real slow through town, careful not to go too fast. I didn't want to draw attention to myself. As I drove through town, I noticed posters on store fronts and lamp posts. I couldn't believe what the posters said:

> EVIE THOMPSON, RUN AWAY. WANTED FOR SUSPICION OF THEFT AND MURDER. IF SPOTTED, CALL THE SHERIFF'S OFFICE RIGHT AWAY.

How dare that Evil Al! Trying to blame everything he did on me!

I held my breath all the way through town. I felt relief because I got through town without seeing a single soul. As I drove through the outskirts of town I decided to go past our house. I felt like I needed one last look at home.

There it was: Mama and Daddy's house, the house they loved and worked so hard for. I vowed that one day I would get our family home back. I would get it back from Evil Al, from the hands of the enemy. As I drove past the house, I saw him, Evil Al walking right out the front door! I was already way past the house, so I don't think he saw me. It just burned me up to think he could just walk right into someone's life and steal what they worked their whole lives to earn. How did he think he could get away with all this meanness?

Well, he wouldn't! I would see to that! I would make him hurt the way he made me hurt!

I realized I was thinking real unclean thoughts against Evil Al. Mama always told me never to hold hate and bitterness in my heart; it would eat you alive. So I asked the Lord above to help me sort through all these bad feelings about Evil Al. This would not be easy, 'cause I could honestly say that I had enough hate for this man to fill all the rivers in the country. I began to pray, and as I prayed I felt a peaceful feeling come over me.

I realized I was smiling. I had not smiled in a long while. I finally felt some hope.

Chapter 12

I drove for miles and miles through the countryside. Once in a while I'd pass a small town and just drive on through. I would need to stop at the next town because I was nearly out of gas. I stopped at a pretty big town called Springfield.

I pulled up at a gas station. A man came up to me and asked, "What can I do you for you, sonny boy?"

"Fill up my tank please, sir."

The man nodded. "Will do."

He kept looking at me the whole time he was putting gas in the truck and washing the windows down. Afterward, he came over to collect the money for the gasoline.

"You look mighty young to be driving around the countryside."

I made my voice sound deep and I told a lie: "I'm sixteen, sir. Everyone in the family runs small."

I handed him the cash, hoping his curiosity was satisfied.

"Uh huh," he nodded and took the money. "Well, thanks for your business."

As I left the gas station, I asked God and Mama to forgive me. The man at the gas station watched me leave. I don't know if he believed what I said, 'cause he still looked mighty suspicious. He either didn't believe I was sixteen or he doubted I was a boy. I needed to get away from that gas station fast. I had a full tank so it would last me awhile.

I went through two more towns: Clinton and Decatur. After I passed through Decatur, I noticed lights flashing! It was a police officer!

There were no other cars around, so I figured it was me that needed to pull over.

Daddy got pulled over once for going too fast. It about gave Mama a heart attack. I didn't think I was speeding; I was sure being careful not to. I pulled off to the side of the road. This big sheriff rolled out of the car. He wasn't so tall, but he sure was round. He had a big round head that seemed to sit right on his shoulders.

Daddy always said, "If you are ever pulled over, act real sorry," so that's what I did.

The sheriff waddled over to the driver's side of the car.

I made a pitiful face and said, "Hey sheriff, I sure am sorry for speeding."

Evie

"You weren't speeding," the sheriff said in a gruff voice.

"Well then, why did you pull me over, sir?"

"I pulled you over because I am mighty suspicious, that's why."

"Why are you suspicious, sir?" I asked.

"I got word there was a vehicle stolen in Peoria by a young kid who may have been in disguise. He may really be a girl. They suspect the girl may have committed murder and is trying to get away. I figured I needed to pull you over and let you prove your innocence. I want you to step out of the truck and drop your drawers, son. One look to prove you got male parts and I'll send you on your way. Either do that or let me see that you don't have titties. Either one, take your pick."

I couldn't believe what I was hearing. He wanted me to pull my pants down or my shirt up! But one look at his grim expression and I knew he wasn't joking. A million thoughts were running through my head. I thought about just gunning Daddy's truck and racing away, but I figured his car probably had more get-up-and-go than Daddy's truck. He would haul me off to jail for sure when he caught me, so that wouldn't work.

As I was thinking these thoughts, I heard the sheriff say, "Are you going to get out? Or am I going to have to pull you out."

I hesitated, which was too long for him. He yanked opened my door and pulled me out of the truck.

"Are you going to pull your britches down yourself or do you want some help?" the sheriff asked with a deep, irritating voice. He sounded like he had snot gurgling at the back of his throat.

He must have made his mind up because all of a sudden ole snotty throat started pulling at my britches. I had to do something quick, so I reared back my right leg and kicked him as hard as I could in the knee.

He hollered a real loud, "Ouch!"

I reached into the truck and grabbed my pouch. I stuffed the key deep in my pocket and took off running as fast as I could into the woods alongside the highway.

The sheriff tried his best to run after me but didn't get far before he tumbled over. If I weren't in such a hurry to get away, I would have taken the time to laugh. It sure was funny to see him tumble over.

"You hood-a-lum!" he yelled. "I'm going to get you and when I do, I'm going to tan your hide!"

Evie

I just kept running and running. I thought I heard gun shots, so I started running zig-zag like a deer again. It reminded me of when Evil Al was after me. I started to get plum out of breath. When I hadn't heard nothing from the direction of the sheriff for a few minutes, I slowed down to a fast walk.

I figured I'd better stay put in these thick woods for a while. I didn't want to run the risk of the big sheriff catching me. I came across a large boulder and decided to sit down for a spell to catch my breath. As I was sitting there, I felt a little sorry for myself.

I really had never done anything wrong—nothing illegal anyway—but here I was being chased like I am some kind of criminal, all because of Evil Al. All of a sudden, the sky became as dark as my thoughts. It was too early for nightfall. Then I felt them: big rain drops. It started with just a few, and then it began to pour. I decided to take my chances and run back to the truck. Surely, the sheriff was gone by now.

It took me a while to run back to the truck. I went a farther distance than I realized. Thankfully, when I got back to the truck the sheriff was nowhere in sight.

I wish I could have waited out the rain, but I knew I had to hurry and get going again before the sheriff came back. He would probably bring help. I started driving down the road. It was sure hard to see with the rain coming down. I thought for sure I was following the road, but I found out real quick I wasn't.

The truck jarred something awful and then came to a complete stop, slamming me into the steering wheel. I ended up in the ditch. Now I was in a real fix. The right side of the truck was about two feet below the left side. I was deep in the ditch. I couldn't move forwards or backwards. I got out of the truck in the pouring rain to see if I could push it out of the ditch. I don't know what I was thinking; the only thing that budged was me. After a lot of useless effort, I collapsed into the muddy ditch, plum worn out.

Finally, I got myself together to get out of the mud, but it was harder than I thought. When I tried to step away, my right foot popped right out of my boots and my sock got all muddy. Then I fell over and my left foot came out of my boots; they were stuck good and proper. It took me a while to dig them out of the thick mud. I sure couldn't put them back on my feet until I washed them off, that's for sure. I was clean worn out by the time I threw myself and my muddy boots back into the truck.

I decided I would at least stay in the truck until the storm passed. I started to shiver. The rain was cold, and I was soaking wet. I remembered Daddy kept a wool blanket behind his seat. I always thought it was scratchy, but right now it felt

Evie

real good against my cold damp skin. The blanket smelled like Daddy.

I sat in Daddy's truck with Daddy's blanket wrapped around me and cried and cried. I missed Daddy so much right now. I wished he could protect me.

Daddy, I'm scared. I don't know what to do.

I prayed a silent prayer for protection. Afterwards, I felt a peaceful feeling that someone was looking out for me. I fell asleep in the crooked truck. I was safe from the rain and I had Daddy wrapped around my shoulders.

I woke up with the sun shining in the truck. I sat up and slid down the seat. I decided I would sit in the floorboard; it was much easier to do that then try to prop myself up into the seat. I was hungry. I had some crackers left, but they had turned into a bunch of soggy crumbs because of the rain. The cheese had mold on it and the apples were all bruised. I figured what I had to eat was better than nothing. I bit off the mold from cheese and spit it out the window. I ate wet cracker crumbs, bites of cheese, and bites of apple. It all actually tasted very good. I realized I was thirsty too. Rain had gathered on parts of Daddy's truck's hood. I had to jump out of the door because of the angle of the truck, but I managed to get myself out. I slurped rainwater from the hood of the truck. I was worn out and muddy and in a real mess, but I laughed at myself, thinking how silly I must look.

With my hunger and thirst satisfied, I figured I'd best be on my way. Staying here in Daddy's lopsided truck would not get me to Grandpa's house. I grabbed my pouch and, making sure everything was inside, tied it around my waist. With compass in hand, I took one last look at Daddy's truck. Then I started walking.

It wasn't easy walking 'cause the ground was so muddy and I had to relieve myself. I had to pee something fierce. I walked about another hour looking for a good place to go. Finally, I decided there was no good place, so I just squatted right where I was, after I made sure no cars were coming, of course. But as soon as I got my pants down and was doing my business, I saw a faint dot of a car coming down the road.

Oh no!

I quickly finished and pulled my pants up. I sure hoped they didn't see what I was doing.

As the car got up alongside me, I noticed it was a bunch of young boys.

One of the boys said, "Hey, did you just take a dump?"

"No!" I shouted. "Well, what were you doing nearly 'sitten on the road with your pants down?" another one of the boys asked.

All the boys were laughing.

"I got hot, and I was resting my legs," I answered him, trying my best to sound like a boy.

"How long you been walking?" another boy asked.

"A long time," I answered.

"Well, hop in," the first boy said, opening the door of the Chevrolet

I figured I might as well. It would save me some walking. They weren't mean boys, just a little ornery that's all. I remember daddy once saying that when you get a bunch of boys together, they are liable to do or say anything.

As I got in the car, the loudest of the four boys said, "Purty puny ain't cha." He grabbed my pouch and said, "What's this, a purse? What are you some kind of sissy boy."

I grabbed the pouch back and everything fell out, so I scrambled to put it all back in.

"Look, he has a compass and food and stuff in the bag. What are you, some kind of hobo or something?"

Another boy took my hat off. "Hey, what kind of silly haircut is this? Did you do it yourself with a handsaw?" All the boys laughed.

I noticed a town up ahead.

"Thanks for the ride. This is where I need to get out. My family lives here," I lied.

"Oh yeah, what family?" the driver asked.

"My dad is the town sheriff," I said, thinking quick. "I'm going to the jail house to see him."

"He's lying," one of the boys said.

"Well, what if he ain't?" another boy said in a nervous whisper. "We don't want him finding out what we got stashed."

Suddenly, they stopped the car and pushed me out.

They sped away so fast I didn't even see which way they went.

Chapter 13

I skinned my knees when they pushed me out of the car. Maybe I shouldn't have lied and told them my daddy was a sheriff. I just wanted them to leave me alone. They had dumped me off in a small town. I think the sign coming in said the name was Assumption. There were only a few buildings: a bank, a grocery store, a barbershop, a café, and a tavern.

I decided to spend some of Mama's money and get me something to eat. The crackers, cheese, and apple were long gone out of my stomach. I sure was hungry. I walked in Sandy's Café and sat down. I didn't eat at cafés much. Mama, Daddy, and me only ate somewhere besides home one other time. Daddy had to go down to Springfield to look at a tractor. Daddy bought the tractor. It didn't cost as much as he had expected, so he had money in his pocket. He was hungry and wanted to take his two lovely ladies out on the town.

I had the most wonderful time! It was the best time I had ever had in my life. We went to place called Midwest Diner. We ordered two fried chicken plates. Mama and me shared. It was good fried chicken, but Daddy and me agreed nobody made fried chicken like Mama did. We told her that too. Mama smiled her real pretty smile, and her face got a little red. I felt real warm and happy inside because I noticed Daddy grabbing Mama's hand under the table.

While I was daydreaming about Mama and Daddy, the waitress came over to my table.

"Hey, sonny boy, what can I get you today?"

I hadn't even looked at the menu in front of me. I didn't know what to order since I wasn't used to cafés, so I just asked her if she had fried chicken.

"Shore do," the big haired, big-breasted waitress named Maudeen said. I knew her name was Maudeen 'cause she had it written on a tag pinned on her chest.

"Do you want the whole dinner or the half dinner?" she asked me.

I didn't know what to say so I just answered, "The whole dinner I guess."

I was really hungry. This meal would have to last me a while.

I must have been a strange sight, cause everybody in the café kept staring at me. The waitress and cook were staring at me the most. I looked down at myself. I did look pitiful.

Evie

Even the clothes that belonged to a twelve-year old boy were hanging on me. I guess all the walking I'd done, and not eating right, had caused me to lose some weight.

The waitress came back to my table without food.

"You going to be able to pay for the food you ordered?" she asked.

Yes, ma'am I will" I answered.

"Are you sure? It's the owner who wants to know. He said you don't look like you have a pot to pee in." She nodded meaningfully at a thick man with thin red hair and freckles. He glared at me real mean-like.

I looked at the waitress and answered her a second time. "Yes, ma'am. I will be able to pay for my fried chicken dinner."

She left with a nod and walked back to the owner. It wasn't any time at all, and she was back at my table without the chicken dinner.

"Sorry, Sonny, the Sandy wants you to pay up 'fore he goes ahead and fries up that chicken. He thinks you might just hightail it out of here after you eat."

This made me *burning* mad! They didn't trust me, and I hadn't given them any reason not to trust me. If I wouldn't have been so blame hungry, I would have just got right up and left.

95

"How much is the dinner?" I asked, trying to keep my voice steady.

"The whole dinner is a dollar seventy-five. A half dinner is seventy-five cents," the waitress answered. She seemed bored with the whole thing.

"I'll have the whole chicken plate just like I told ya." I reached in my pocket, pulled out my money, and gave her the five-dollar bill. Her whole face came to life when she saw the money.

She took hold of it with both hands and muttered under her breath, "Well I'll be. I'll be back with your change."

I watched her walk up to the owner and slap the money down in front of him. I got the feeling she didn't like Mr. Sandy making me pay first. I bet no other customer had to pay first.

I finally got my chicken plate. I got three pieces of chicken, creamed potatoes, green beans, and apple sauce. It all tasted so good.

I must have been eating fast' cause when Maudeen filled up my water glass she said, "You better come up for air, son."

Then she walked away laughing. I didn't finish eatin' one of the chicken pieces 'cause I wanted to take it with me. I wrapped it in a paper napkin and stuck it in my pouch. Maudeen asked me if I had room for pie and said she would give me a piece on the house. I didn't know quite what she meant; I was imagined eating pie on a house.

She noticed I was puzzled and chuckled. "I am giving you the pie. I feel bad Sandy gave you such a hard time."

"Does Sandy mind if you give me a piece of pie?" I asked.

"Oh, who cares if he does or not," Maudeen answered. I was plum full, but I couldn't turn down pie, especially being that it was free and all. "It's mighty nice of you, ma'am. I'd sure love some pie."

"All right, then. Because you are getting it free, you can't be picky. We have some extra custard, so that's what it has to be."

"Sounds mighty good to me, ma'am," I answered.

"Oh, don't be calling me ma'am. Just call me Maudeen."

"Yes, ma'am. I mean, Miss Maudeen."

Maudeen seemed like such a nice a lady. I decided when she came back with my pie, I would ask her where I could get on a train.

When I did, she laughed. "Sonny you ain't from around here, are you? We don't have no trains coming through here. We do have a bus though. You'll have to wait until morning. I think the last run was about one hour ago. Next run will be about seven in the morning."

"Thank you," I said in a quiet voice. I put my head down in disappointment.

"Are you ok, sonny boy? You seem mighty down in the dumps right now. Do you have kin folk that care about you?"

"Yes, ma'am—I mean Maudeen—I'm heading to my grandfather's house," I explained as I ate the custard pie quickly. Even amid my disappointment, the pie was delicious.

This seemed to satisfy her curiosity about me.

She smiled and said, "Well, good. Now, you take care of yourself, and thank you for stopping in."

I thanked her and left the café feeling much better after eating.

I walked around the town looking for the bus stop. I couldn't see where a bus stop would be. As I was looking around the town, a kind old lady asked me if I was lost. I told her I was looking for the bus stop. With a crooked finger, she pointed to the general store.

Atop the store was a sign that said Assumption Mercantile. Out front was a long, old, unpainted bench that I'm sure could give you splinters as long as your finger. When I walked into the store, many smells hit me at once. I smelled a mixture of dust, cinnamon, and soap. Somehow, the mixture

Evie

of all those smells was strangely comforting. I was greeted by the store clerk. He was a little man with glasses worn down on his nose.

"Hi, son, what can I do you for today?"

"I need to buy a bus ticket," I answered.

"You must be the new lad in town everyone is talking about. I hear you have a pocket full of money. Well, you came to the right place. I have plenty you can spend that money on."

"Thank you, sir. I would just like a bus ticket."

"Well, there won't another bus to come through here until seven in the morning."

"It's ok. I'll wait," I answered, anxious for him to just take my money and give me the ticket. He took a roll of tickets, tore one off, and handed it to me. I reached in my pocket and counted out one dollar and seventy-five cents.

As he took my money, he asked, "So you're going to Carbondale, huh?"

"Yes sir," I answered.

He looked like he wanted to ask me more questions, but the door opened and three women with a slew of young ones walked in. He was quickly distracted. One of the women was dragging a little girl and what looked to be an eight-year-old boy behind her.

The boy looked at me with a no-good look on his face and blurted out, "Hey! You must be that goofy boy who ate at Sandy's. Daddy told me about you."

The mother quickly grabbed her son by the top of his ear and said, "Timothy, hush your mouth!"

I walked out of the store and figured I'd better just make up my mind that this old bench was where I'd be spending the night; I didn't have anywhere else to go. So, I sat on the smoothest part of the bench and just watched the townspeople. I saw all three women leave with all their children trailing behind. The rude boy stuck out his tongue as he walked away.

People came and went out of the little general store. The town was small enough that I could see all the buildings. I saw a man get pulled out of the tavern and taken to jail by the town sheriff. I saw boys playing stick ball in the road until a woman came out of the dress shop and shooed them on their way.

As the hour went by, the town activity got less and less. The clerk from the general store came out and locked the door behind him. He looked my way, shook his head, and went the other direction. It was getting dark. The only lights I saw came from the café. I was alone with my thoughts. I thought of many things: of Mama and Daddy, of Evil Al, and of the Smiths. I thought of how proud Mama would be of me when I finally got to grandpa's house.

After a while, I began feeling mighty sleepy. I laid down on the bench. I put my pouch under my head and fell asleep. While I slept, I dreamed that someone was pulling at my pockets. I woke up to the smell of whiskey. I knew the smell because whenever I got a cough Mama would give me a dose. She said her daddy used whiskey for medicine too.

I opened my eye to see a big man with whiskers covering his face. He had so much whiskey in him he couldn't even stand up straight.

"Get your filthy hands off me," I screamed.

"I will after I reach in here and get all that money," he slurred. "I saw you stuff it in your britches."

As I took a closer look at him, I remembered seeing him sitting at the counter in the café. He didn't look quit as wild-looking in the café in the middle of the day. He was drunk but he was strong: he held me down with one arm and reached into my pocket with his other. He pulled out all the money I had left.

"Hey! Give me back my money!" I yelled, pulling at the drunken man's arm.

"What's going on over there?" I heard a male voice shout.

101

I looked over and saw Sandy the café owner and Maudeen the waitress. They were locking up the café.

"He stole my money!" I yelled.

"Ralph, leave that kid alone and give him his money back!" Maudeen bellowed.

"This ain't his money. It's my money" the drunk slurred, my cash in his hands.

"You ain't got no money," Maudeen answered. The drunk shoved the money down the front of his pants.

"Sorry kid," Sandy said after an awkward pause. "I ain't going down there for your money. You're going to have to take this up with the law. The sheriff's office is down the street, three building to your left."

"Sandy, we just can't leave this boy alone penniless. He was on his way to meet up with his grandpa. How is he supposed to get there without money?"

Sandy pulled two silver dollars from his pocket and said, "Here you go, kid, maybe this will help you to get where you want to go." He tossed me the dollars. Then he patted me on the shoulder and said, "Go on down to the sheriff's office. He might be able to get you your money back. If you do get it back," he added meaningfully. "I'd sure give a good washing before I touched it."

"Best of luck, son," Maudeen said kindly.

Evie

I knew there was no way I was going to get my money back because I couldn't go to the sheriff. He was liable to get suspicious and ask me a bunch of questions. I had no choice but to use the few dollars Sandy had given me and let the bus take me as far as it would on two dollars, which wasn't going to be far.

I laid down on the bench again, just thinking about how Mama's hard-saved money was gone at the hands of a no-good drunk. The money Mama worked so hard to save was going to be wasted on whiskey. Once again, I did the only thing I knew to do when I was in a heap of trouble.

I prayed. "Dear Lord, please help me get to grandpa's house. As you know, I don't have hardly any money to get me there. I'm going to have to count on you to help me."

The prayer must have relaxed me some because I fell asleep.

I woke up to the sound of the bus and people gathering around. I quickly grabbed my pouch and felt in my pocket for my money—then I remembered I know longer had Mama's money. Just the two dollars Sandy gave me. My heart became heavy, but then I remembered I had to put my trust in the Lord above.

I had to relieve myself, but it looked like the bus would be leaving soon so I climbed up the steps to board. I had never been on a bus before. It was scary and exciting all at the same time. I sat next to a lady. As soon as I sat beside her, she held her nose and moved to another seat. It had been a while since I had a bath. I didn't realize I was stinking already. I started sniffing under my arms. I guess all the sweatin' I was doing while walking had caused me to stink some. A whiff of the cold fried chicken in my pouch didn't help matters none. It embarrassed the tar out of me to think I made someone move because of the way I smelled. Mama always taught me how important keeping clean was.

"Sorry, Mama," I said under my breath. "I just can't help it. I'll take a good bath first chance I get."

I did hate being dirty, and this binding around my chest was itching something awful.

I looked around the bus, I was the only one with a seat to myself. I noticed an old woman behind me. She was knitting with glasses on and would peer over them to look at me. I tried to smile but she didn't smile back. Across from me was a young couple. I figured they just got married: they were sitting real close holding hands and staring at each other. Sometimes the man would whisper something in her ear, and she would laugh this silly little laugh. Behind the couple was a girl a little younger than me, sitting proper-like with her hands folded on her lap. Beside her was a neatly dressed lady. I bet it was her Mama.

I found myself feeling real envious of that girl. I noticed the woman trying to talk to the girl, but the girl wanted no part of it. I wanted to tell the girl she better listen to her mama 'cause there might come a day she won't have her to listen to. I wanted to tell her I could never hear my Mama's voice again except for in my mind. I guess I was staring, cause the girl looked in my direction and gave me a real mean look. I summed up the situation right then and there: the girl was spoiled rotten.

"Be careful, girl," I said under my breath. "One day it could all be taken away from you, and you'll be left with nothing."

When the bus finally came to a stop, the driver shouted, "Carbondale!"

A few people stood up to get off the bus, but most were staying on for Memphis. I wish I had the money to continue, but I didn't. Somehow, I would have to find a way.

The girl and her mom stayed seated. As I walked down the center aisle, I suddenly felt something in front of my foot, and then I fell hard on my knees. The spoiled girl had stuck her foot out to trip me. Picking myself up off the bus floor, I glared at the girl. She was laughing. Her mama had seen what she did, but wasn't even scolding her.

"Why did you trip me?" I shouted. "I didn't do anything to you!"

"Because you are a smelly, weird-looking boy and I wanted to see you fall," the bratty girl answered in a hateful voice.

If I weren't mistaken, I think I saw her mama snicker too. No wonder the girl was a brat. Her mama didn't train her right.

"Thank you, Mama, for loving me enough to train me right," I said to myself as I limped off the bus.

Chapter 14

*I*t was about noon when I got off the bus. I looked around the town of Carbondale. It was a little bigger than Assumption. The town had a friendly feel. The first thing I needed to do was find a place to relieve myself. I had to pee so bad I felt like I would pop. I noticed a few outhouses behind some buildings. I ran to the closest one, opened the door, sat down, and relieved myself. I think it took me five long minutes to empty. I sure did feel better. I grabbed my pouch and walked out of the outhouse.

"Lord, where do I go now?" I prayed.

I roamed around town. I felt I was going in circles just waiting for something to happen, only I didn't know what. I was feeling tired, itchy, and hungry. I guess I felt pretty miserable. I looked down the road and noticed a little church on the edge of town. The church had large steps in front of it. I decided to sit on the steps and eat the piece of chicken I saved from the café. The chicken was now hard. All the crusty coating had fallen off. The chicken was left with a yucky grease coating on it. It was all I had. I tried nibbling on it the best I could. It was just too hard to eat, so I tossed it in the bushes by the church. Some hungry animal would be real happy to eat it. I laid down on the steps of the church and started telling God all my troubles like He didn't know them already.

I didn't know it then, but a man around the corner was listening to me tell all my troubles to God. It turned out the man was the pastor of the church.

He came around the corner and said, "Hi son! I'm Brother John Sanders. What's your name?"

Oh no! He wanted to know my name! I really had not given any thought to what my "boy" name should be, so I just blurted out my daddy's name.

"I'm J.C. Thompson," I said.

I took one look in his eyes and knew he was a real preacher. He was a real man of God, not some imposter like Evil Al.

"Well, hi there, J.C.," he said. "Glad to meet you."

"Glad to meet you too, sir," I said, hoping he would not ask me any more questions.

"I couldn't help overhearing: it sounds like you are in somewhat of a predicament."

"Well, yes sir," I said, getting flushed that he had overheard me. "I'm traveling to my grandpa's. He lives in

Trenton, Tennessee. I had all the money it would take me to get there, but a drunk stole it."

It sounded like I was telling Brother Sander's a tall tale even though every word I said was true. If he doubted me, he didn't show it.

He looked at me with kind eyes and said, "J.C., myself and my wife and son Colby would be honored to have you join us for dinner."

"Oh Brother Sanders, thank you so much for the invitation but I'm not fit to enter your house as filthy as I am. I would be mighty grateful for a little food handed to me out the door, but then I should be on my way."

"Well, young lad, why do you think you are not fit?"

"The truth is I have not had the chance to properly bath. I've conjured up quite the odor I'm afraid."

The nice young preacher smiled at me and said, "Considering your predicament, I would like to offer you a bath. You may take it before dinner if you feel more comfortable."

Being that I was itchy on every part of my body, I was desperate enough to accept the invitation this nice man was offering me.

His house was just a short walk from the church. He told me to wait outside for just a moment so he could inform his wife. Seconds later, Brother Sanders opened his front door. Standing beside him was a very pretty, small lady holding the cutest little boy I ever laid eyes on.

"J.C., I'd like you to meet my lovely wife, Beth, and our son, Colby."

"Hi!" I nodded curtly. "Pleased to meet you, ma'am and Colby."

Beth smiled sweetly. "Please come in."

Their home was very pretty and clean. There seemed to be pictures of flowers everywhere. Mama would like these people and their home, I thought to myself.

Beth Sanders asked me to follow her. She showed me the bathroom and put out a washcloth, towel, and soap for me. I was very grateful the Sander's had running water. I began running my bathwater. I took off my clothes and then began the task of unwrapping the binding on my chest. To my horror, I had developed a rash. No wonder I was itching so much.

It felt so wonderful to get into the water. The rash stung something fierce at first, but then the cool water soothed my aching skin. It felt so wonderful in the water that I didn't want to leave the bath. I realized if I didn't get out soon the Sanders would wonder if I had drowned. I slowly got out of the tub and dried myself off, being careful to only pat the rash dry. As I patted the rash dry, I noticed there were places on my skin where I was actually bleeding.

I picked up the cloth I used for binding. It had yellowed from sweat. I could not put that filthy rag back against my skin for fear of getting an infection. I would just have to take my chances that no one would notice my chest. I drained the bathtub to get rid of the embarrassing muddy brown water I had left behind. Then I ran a little fresh water to clean the pure dirt left in the bathtub. I vowed then and there I would never let myself get dirty again.

Suddenly, I heard a rap on the door.

"Are you okay?"

It was Beth.

"I'm fine, Ma'am!" I answered. "I'll be out in a minute."

I reached into my pouch and got the other pair of pants and shirt I had taken from the Smiths' house. They were mighty wrinkled. The pants had a little grease on them from the chicken I put in the pouch, but at least they were in better shape than the clothes I had just taken off. When I glanced down at the dirty heap of clothes on the floor, I wondered again how I could have stood my own filthiness. I folded the clothes up the best I could and hid the filthy binding in between them. Not knowing what else to do with the dirty clothes, I left them in the corner of the bathroom. I would have stuffed them back into my pouch had they not been so smelly. Maybe I could wash them somehow, I thought, or maybe they were too far gone to come clean.

Somehow, I would have to make it to Grandpa's with the clothes on my back, unless God saw fit to give me more.

Chapter 15

I left the bathroom and walked into the kitchen. When John and Beth looked up from their conversation and saw me, they gave me a strange look. Then I realized I had forgotten to put my hat back on, and my hair had grown out quite a bit since I cut it at the Smiths' house. The mud that I always made sure was smeared on my face was also gone. Somehow, I felt my secret was out. But if they knew, they didn't say anything.

We all sat down at the table. Beth put Colby in a highchair. He babbled all kinds of sounds and nibbled on a cracker. Beth placed a steamy hot bowl of beef stew in front of me and a piece of corn bread.

"Thank you, kindly," I said.

"It is our pleasure, J.C. John told me how he couldn't help but overhear your prayer for help, you poor dear," Beth said, with sincere compassion in her voice.

Brother John sat down at the table next to Beth he gently took her hand and softly said, "Shall we say grace?"

He bowed his head. We all did the same.

"Dear Lord, thank you for the food that you have supplied. Thank you for loving us and looking out for our every need. We thank you for bringing us a very special house guest."

My eyes misted over as Brother John thanked the Lord for me.

"Are you ok?" Beth asked tenderly.

"Yes, Ma'am," I muttered. We all ate in silence. I was so hungry. The stew tasted delicious!

After a few minutes of eating, the Sanders began asking me questions. I didn't want to lie to them because they were so nice, but I knew I couldn't tell them my whole story, only part of it. They asked me where Grandpa lived. They asked about Mama and Daddy. I told them about Daddy's farm accident. I told them Mama hit her head and died.

Again, Beth said, "You poor dear."

I guess I started acting uncomfortable. I felt myself squirming in my seat. When they stopped asking questions, I was very relieved.

After lunch, I played with Colby while Beth did the dishes. Brother John said he needed to do some visiting; he mentioned that a few church members needed prayer. Before he left, he invited me to stay the night so I could be rested before I continued on my journey to Grandpa's house. It was

Evie

mighty tempting, but I knew I needed to be on my way. The longer I stayed here, the longer it would take me to get to Grandpa's. I needed to fulfill Mama's plan, Mama's last wish.

I explained to them I really needed to be on my way. I really hated to ask, but I would need food for my journey, so I swallowed my pride and ask if they could spare any food.

"Of course! I wouldn't think of letting you leave without food," Beth said.

She began gathering food in the kitchen. I laid my pouch on the table to put food in.

Beth considered my pouch and said, "How about I give you a new satchel. That one looks like it has been through a lot."

I looked at my pouch. It was dirty and grease stained. Without waiting for my answer, she went into another room and came out with a long leather handle bag.

"Oh, I couldn't take something that nice," I told her.

She waved my protest away. "It is perfectly fine. We weren't using it. Besides, I always like to send our quests home with a gift."

"Thank you so much," I answered.

I began emptying my things out of the dirty pouch and putting them in the nice leather satchel. Beth looked on as I emptied one bag and filled the other.

She noticed my compass. "Did your compass come in handy?"

"Yes, ma'am, it did."

Brother John came into the kitchen to say goodbye. "J.C., are you sure you can't stay a little longer? We would love to have you around for a few days."

"Thank you, Brother John, but I really do need to be on my way."

"Ok then. May God go before you and protect you and guide your every step."

He shook my hand and walked towards the door. When he opened it, he was met by the town sheriff.

"Hello, sheriff," I heard John say. "What can I do for you today?"

"Well, I was wondering if you have seen a young lad about yay tall? Scrawny, funny-looking haircut. Possibly a girl dressed as a boy?"

"Oh no!" I breathed as I grabbed the leather satchel. "Miss Beth, thank you for everything. I have to go."

I ran to the backdoor while Beth yelled after me, "J.C., I haven't fixed your sandwiches yet!"

I didn't have time to answer. I needed to get away fast. I wrenched their back door open, but I felt a strong arm grab me.

Evie

It was Brother John.

"The sheriff's gone!" he said. "I sent him on his way. I told him I had not seen a girl dressed as a boy because you are a boy, aren't you, J.C.? At least. as far as I can tell."

I could not tell if Brother John felt sorry for me or was annoyed with me. He still had a grip on me as he brought me back into the house. Miss Beth was holding Colby, watching everything with wide eyes.

Brother John sat me down on the chair and said, "Ok let's hear it. Tell me why the law is after you. Why are you running?"

Beth went into the other room to put Colby down for a nap. I sat in silence. When Beth came back into the room, she joined her husband on the sofa, looking very concerned.

Brother John continued, "J.C., Beth and I want to help you, but I have a feeling there are a lot of things you are not telling us."

John paused for time and asked, "You don't want us in trouble with the law for housing a criminal, do you?"

I looked at Brother John. He was looking at me in stern yet sympathetic way. I looked over at Miss Beth. She was nodding her head slightly, as if to encourage me to speak. I sat still, not knowing where to begin.

Miss Beth cleared her throat and said in a kind, quiet voice, "We know you are not a boy." She and John exchanged glances. "I realized you were a girl the moment you walked into our home. I figured you had a good reason to be in disguise. I shared my suspicions with John. He wasn't convinced until you came out of the bathroom."

I just sat there with my head down. I felt plum foolish. How did I think I could fool people? Brother John spoke again, "So how about telling us what your real name is?"

"Evie," I whispered.

"What's that?" Brother John asked, learning closer.

"My name is Evelyn Thompson," I spoke up. "Evie for short."

"Ok, Evie, we are making progress. How about telling us the rest of your story?" John asked. I shook my head. I just couldn't bring myself to tell them the horrible things I have been through.

Brother John stood up and went to the door.

"Where are you going, John?" Miss Beth asked.

"I'm going to get the sheriff. If Evie doesn't want to tell us why the law is after her, maybe the law can tell us why they are after her."

"No!" I shouted! "I'll tell you."

Brother John sat back down and looked at me sternly. "Ok, but we want the honest truth. No lies in this house."

I had a feeling Brother John would not have really gone to the sheriff, but because I wasn't completely sure, I figured the best thing to do was to go ahead and tell him everything. I figured I'd just start from the beginning.

I looked at Brother John, then at Miss Beth. I sighed, knowing it would be hard remembering and telling all the hard things that I have gone through. I leaned back on the chair and began my story. I told them about Mama and Daddy, about what wonderful loving parents they both were. I told them about Daddy's accident and how hard it was on Mama and me. How we missed him so and tried to keep the farm going on our own. I told them about how Mama met and married Brother Al Jenkins. He turned out not to be the man of God that Mama and the townspeople thought he was. I told them that he had Mama fooled in the beginning, but after they were already married Mama began to realize what I already knew: Al Jenkins was an evil man. I told them how Mama and me came up with a plan to get away from him, but before we had a chance Evil Al killed her.

This bit of news caused the Sanders to be wide-eyed and opened-mouthed with shock. I waited a few minutes for them to get over what I had just said, and then I continued. I explained to them about the Smiths and how evil Al killed them too, and how he was trying to blame me.

"Evil Al took everything from me," I cried.

Miss Beth handed me a hanky and encouraged me to continue. I told them how he took Mama, my home, and my friends. Now he was trying to take my freedom.

After I had said all this, I sat silent, relieved that it was all out. I didn't tell every little detail, but I said enough. They listened real close to everything I had said. Every so often Miss Beth would dab a tissue on her eyes. I think she felt real sorry for me, because she ended up sitting on the chair with her arms around me.

"Whew!" Brother John said. "You have been through quite a lot young lady. If what you are telling me is true, you will have the law after you until you defend yourself. My suggestion to you is to get yourself a good lawyer. I'm going to some checking up on this Al Jenkins character to see what I can find out. Meanwhile, I know you want to get to your grandfather's house. This has been a big day. Why don't you spend the night here tonight? If you set out on foot right now, you are sure to be caught. I haven't talked to Beth, but maybe we could drive you to your grandpa's," Brother John said as he looked at Beth.

Evie

"Of course," Miss Beth said with a smile. Then, as if to lighten the mood, she added, "I am always up for a road trip."

I couldn't believe my ears! Brother John and Miss Beth were going to drive me to Grandpa's, all the way to Trenton, Tennessee. I felt so grateful it was hard for me to talk. The tears would not stop flowing down my face.

"Thank you so kindly. Thank you so kindly," I kept saying.

Miss Beth came over to me and hugged me and said, "We feel God brought you to our doorstep. It is our pleasure to help you."

Brother John clasped his hands together and said, "Well, now that we have gotten to the bottom of things, I need to do some visiting that I intended to do much earlier."

He walked to the door, turned around, and winked. "I would stay in the house if I were you. We don't need anyone spotting our little outlaw."

"Don't worry, John. Evie and I won't be going outside. I've got some ideas to keep us real busy in the house," Beth said with a smile.

Brother John smiled back. "Ok, I'll see you at dinner."

I wondered what ideas Miss Beth had. I looked at her with a questioning look in my eyes.

"Evie, you don't have to be in disguise anymore," Miss Beth declared.

"You are right, Miss Beth. I don't, do I?"

"Follow me." We went into her bedroom, and she took several dresses out of her closet. "Try these on see which one fits."

"Oh, Miss Beth, I couldn't take your pretty dress."

"Nonsense. I like to sew. I have more dresses than I need. Here, try this one on. It will look real pretty with your hair color."

I held the dress up. "Miss Beth, this dress is so little it won't even come near fitting me."

"Evie, you are small. Remove your clothes so we can try it."

I began taking off my clothes.

"Oh, Evie, you need a brassiere," Miss Beth said caringly.

She handed me one of her brassieres. I had never worn a brassiere before. I guess the reason being is I didn't need one before Mama died. It just seemed like all of a sudden, my chest grew. It felt a little strange to me, especially since I had been bound up for a while.

Miss Beth looked down at the boy underwear I had on, and without saying a word she handed me a pair of white lace panties. She respectively turned around and faced the other direction while I put on the fresh underclothes. How wonderful it felt to wear something girlie again. After putting on the underclothes, I slipped the pretty, light-yellow dress over my head. Miss Beth buttoned the back buttons, and to my surprise the dress fit perfect.

Miss Beth smiled and said, "You are beautiful, Evie."

I felt my face get warm. I had never thought of myself as beautiful before. Miss Beth brushed my hair and got a ribbon and tied it around my head. I walked towards the full-length mirror in the corner of the bedroom.

"Wait," Miss Beth said. "Let me do one more thing before you look at yourself."

She put cheek and lip color on me.

"Mama used to put this on her face," I said softly.

"Your Mama must have been a beautiful lady inside and out."

"She was," I answered, looking down.

"Come now," Miss Beth said, wanting to cheer me up. "Look at yourself."

I knew it was me standing in front of the mirror, but I could not believe it. I truly felt like I was staring at someone else in the mirror. I looked like Mama. I looked like the picture she had of herself on her bedroom dresser when her and Daddy first got married.

"What do you think?" Miss Beth asked.

"I look a whole lot better," I answered. We both laughed. At the moment, we heard Colby crying out for his mama.

We spent the afternoon playing with Colby and making dinner together. I couldn't remember having a better time. It felt so good to have fun. I had not had fun for a long, long time.

Brother Sanders walked in and declared that dinner smelled delicious. When Brother John saw me, his mouth opened and closed, and then opened and closed again.

Miss Beth went over to him and playfully put her arm around him.

"Honey," she said, "meet the new Miss Evelyn Thompson."

"Oh my goodness! I would have not recognized you, Evie. I'll say one thing for sure: that grandfather of yours better own a rifle to keep the young men away."

I smiled, feeling embarrassed, never thinking a boy would even give me a second thought.

We all sat down and enjoyed a wonderful dinner. Miss Beth made chicken and dumplings. It was the best chicken and dumplings I ever ate. Brother John hugged Miss Beth and

Evie

thanked her for the wonderful dinner. I'm ashamed to admit it, but I felt envy. Miss Beth sure was lucky to have such a nice home and nice family and all. No one deserved it more than her. Someday I would have it too, God willing, but first I had to prove my innocence and keep out of jail.

The ride to Grandpa's was long. I thanked the Sanders over and over for taking me. It was a full day's drive. They knew the ride would be hard on Colby, so Miss Beth asked one of the ladies from church to take care of him while they made the trip. They assured me this was a little vacation for them.

"Lord, I don't think you created finer folks than the Sanders," I thought.

We finally got to Trenton, Tennessee, the town Grandpa lived in. It was real confusing the way Mama described where Grandpa's house was. Before we found it, we mistakenly stopped at a neighbor's house thinking it was Grandpa's. When we went to the door and realized the person living there wasn't Grandpa, we asked them if they knew where William Owens lived.

"Oh yeah, I know where William Owens lives. About five houses down in that direction," the older man said as he pointed down the street. "Glad to see he has some company. He sticks to himself since Mabel died. That was his second wife you know. She died about a year or so ago."

"Thank you for the directions," I said.

"Hey," the older man hollered after me. "You must be kin to ole Bill. You look just like his daughter, Laura. She up and left years ago. Don't know that she has been back for a while."

I didn't tell him who I was. Didn't figure he needed to know. He seemed like a man who gathered information and was eager to spread it.

The Sanders had waited in the car for me. I told them where the old man said Grandpa lived. I told them how the neighbor told me Grandpa's second wife died a year or so ago.

"When did you lose your maternal grandmother?" Brother John wondered. I figured I'd been honest with them about everything else, so I might as well be honest about this too.

"I know this is going to sound strange," I began, "but my grandmother wasn't my grandmother at all. It turns out after reading Mama's letter that my grandmother was my mama. My Mama, well, who I thought was my Mama, was actually my sister, and my grandpa is my real daddy. My real mama died giving birth to me. My real daddy who I consider my grandpa was so sad about his wife dying that he wasn't able to take care of a baby, so he gave me to his older daughter Laura. The way I figure it, my Mama who was really my sister couldn't have babies of her own, so she felt real blessed to raise me. She moved away so it would not be hard on Grandpa. As far as my heart and my thinking goes, my Daddy and Mama who raised me are my real Daddy and Mama and Grandpa is Grandpa. I know all this must sound confusing. You can imagine how shocked and confused I was when I first read this in mama's letter."

    Brother John and Miss Beth were looking at me with big wide eyes the whole time I was telling the story. Brother John's mouth opened and closed the same way it did when he first saw me looking like a girl. Miss Beth got her hanky out of her purse and started wiping her eyes again.

    Brother John cleared his throat and said, "Young lady, you have been through more in your young lifetime than most people have in two lifetimes. There is a reason for it, though you may not know it yet. But you'll find out sooner or later."

    When the neighbor had pointed down the road about five houses away, he didn't mention miles between each house. I guess the drive gave me a chance to tell the Sanders a little more about myself.

    We finally pulled up to Grandpa's house. The house was old but neat and tidy. Many emotions hit me upon seeing it. Mainly, I felt relief.

With tears filling my eyes, I whispered, "Mama, I made it. I made it to Grandpa's. I stuck to our plan."

Chapter 16

We all got out of the car. I looked from Brother John to Miss Beth and felt a swell of emotion in my chest. I really felt like the Sanders were like family. They seemed to really care for me. You know how you can just tell when someone cares for you. They cared without knowing me for very long, or very well. I just knew God meant for us to meet. This was a meet-up made in heaven. I felt a ray of hope that things might just work out after all.

I went up to Grandpa's door with a smile on my face. I knocked, but there was no answer. Brother John knocked a more powerful knock. We waited a while. Finally, Grandpa opened the door. He was an old man with white hair. His face still looked handsome. I thought to myself that he must have been very handsome when he was a young man.

He looked at me and said, "Laura?" He studied my face. "No, you are not Laura."

"No sir, I am not. I am Laura's daughter, Evelyn." As I said those words, a bunch of emotions showed up on

Grandpa's face. He stumbled over his words and then finally said, "Well come on in and sit down."

He looked questioning at Brother John and Miss Beth. I introduced them as my friends. It felt real good to introduce them that way.

"Pleased to meet you," he said. "Please come in and have a seat."

As soon as we sat down, Grandpa asked where my mother was. I don't know why, but the question surprised me. Of course, he would ask about Mama. He didn't know she had died. No one told him. I should have tried to get in touch with him before I started my journey, but I was too busy getting away from Evil Al. The only way I knew to tell Grandpa was just to tell him.

"Grandpa, Mama died."

Grandpa's eyes went wide with surprise and dismay.

"No! No! No!" he kept saying. His eyes filled with tears.

"How did this happen?" he asked me in a whisper.

Suddenly, I felt Miss Beth by my side. She put her arms gently around me. Brother John went to Grandpa's side. Grandpa looked in my eyes, eager for an explanation about his daughter's death.

"She fell and hit her head on the bed post," I answered.

Evie

I remembered the letter Mama had written for Grandpa. I reached in the leather pouch and got it. The letter was all crinkled. I tried my best to smooth it out. I handed the letter to Grandpa. He took it from me like it was a fragile piece of glass. He opened it and read the letter. Grandpa broke down and sobbed and sobbed. Brother John sat by his side, holding and comforting him.

After several minutes, Grandpa gathered himself together. He looked at me in a real sympathetic way and said, "Laura asked if you could live with me, but I don't know for sure if that's the best thing. My health hasn't been very good lately and I'm not used to having young ones around."

Panic began to fill me. I almost felt like I couldn't breathe. *Did I come all this way for Grandpa to turn me away?* We all sat quiet for a moment with our own thoughts.

Grandpa cleared his throat. "Well, I guess you aren't really a young one anymore. You are getting older. Did you ever give any thought to just staying on at your own home? I mean the one that belonged to your folks."

Because Grandpa asked me that question, I knew Mama had not mentioned she had gotten married again. It made me start to wonder if Grandpa knew that Daddy died.

"Grandpa did Mama tell you about Daddy dying?"

131

"Yes, child. She notified me after he died, but it happened right after I lost my wife Mabel. I was also down in my back so I couldn't make to the funeral. I sure wish I could have been there for her though. I can't help but wonder if things would have been different if I had been there."

Grandpa looked puzzled for a minute and then asked, "She hit her head on the bedpost, huh? That sounds mighty peculiar. Folks don't normally die just because they hit their head. I wonder what made her fall. She was always such a graceful girl. It just doesn't make any sense to me at all." Grandpa seemed to be thinking out loud.

Brother John spoke up. "Mr. Owens, Evie has much more to tell you about her life. Maybe we can just sit back relax a while and let Evie continue filling you in on her life."

"Well, that makes sense, but before we do let me put together some dinner for us. You folks traveled so far. I'm sure you worked up and appetite. I don't have much, but I'll give you what I've got. Mabel was so good at these types of things. Lord knows I miss her."

"Mr. Owens, you need not bother. We didn't eat that awful long ago," Miss Beth said.

"No, I insist you folks need to eat," Grandpa said as he stood up and walked hunched-over to the kitchen.

Evie

"That's sure nice of you, Mr. Owens, Actually, a little food sounds really good to me right now," Brother John said with a good-natured grin on his face.

"You men are always hungry," Miss Beth joked. "Well, at least let me help you."

"Never turn down good help in the kitchen," Grandpa, responded good-naturedly.

Suddenly, a lighthearted mood replaced the sad mood we all felt only moments ago. For this I was grateful.

Brother John and me spent time talking and praying while Miss Beth and Grandpa were in the kitchen. A short time later, Grandpa called us into the kitchen. We sat down to fried bacon, scrambled eggs, and biscuits. This was food I usually had in the morning, but I wasn't going to complain because I could eat breakfast food all day long.

"Brother John," Grandpa said, "you have yourself a keeper. She a little whirlwind in the kitchen."

"Oh, believe me. I know," Brother John said with a wink in Miss Beth's direction.

We ate our meal, enjoying each other's company while we talked about simple things like the weather and Grandpa's dog and Colby. After dinner, Miss Beth and me cleaned up the kitchen while Brother John and Grandpa walked around the farm.

Later, we all gathered back in the sitting room.

Grandpa spoke up and said, "Well, Evie, tell your grandpa all the things I need to hear."

I began, "After Daddy died, Mama and me tried real hard to keep the farm going. We just couldn't do all the work on our own. It was just too much."

Grandpa nodded.

"About this time, the new preacher started coming over. He would come over and ask a whole heap of questions, and before I could turn around twice, Mama and the preacher were courting. Then before long they got married."

If Grandpa was surprised, he didn't show it. But I could tell he didn't like what I was telling him.

"So, you did not approve of your Mama marrying the new preacher?" Grandpa asked.

"No sir I did not" I answered firmly back.

"And this preacher now has possession of your folk's home?" Grandpa asked.

Before I could answer Grandpa, Brother John spoke up and said, "Evie I think you need to your Grandpa the *whole* story."

Brother John made the word whole seem a mile long. I nodded in agreement.

Evie

Between the three of us, we told Grandpa my story. The only thing we left out was that I knew Grandpa was really my father. Grandpa sat quiet through the whole story, listening intently. Sometimes he looked real angry, sometimes he looked sad, and other times he would tear up.

He finally spoke up and shouted, "All this just ain't right! It ain't right at all, I tell you! This Al Jenkins took everything from my daughters! He should be stopped in his tracks! He should be put away somewhere where he can't do anybody any harm, I tell you!"

"Mr. Owens, I assure you I'm going to do everything in my power to see that justice is served," Brother John said firmly.

Grandpa nodded in agreement.

He turned to me with compassion in his eyes. "Child, you have been through enough. You need a place to lay your head. You stay here with me."

"Oh, thank you so much, Grandpa!" I shouted as I hugged Grandpa's neck. Being with Grandpa is exactly where Mama wanted me to be. Besides, there was nowhere else for me to go. I could not imagine where I would go if Grandpa truly didn't want me.

"Ok, let's go to the car and get your belongings since you'll be staying a while," Grandpa said.

"I have no belongings, Grandpa, except for this leather satchel Miss Beth gave me and the things I have in it. Miss Beth was kind enough to give me this dress I have on. I have the boy's clothes I told you about in the satchel."

"Well, ok then. We'll just make do, won't we?" Grandpa said.

I smiled at Grandpa, feeling good I was with family again.

"Evie, dear, we need to be on our way. We need to get back to Colby," Brother John said. "We will keep you in our prayers and will be checking on you often."

Miss Beth gave me a big hug and said that I seemed like a little sister to her, and she would cherish the times we spent together. My eyes stung with tears. I truly loved these people and silently prayed that I would see them again someday.

Chapter 17

Grandpa and I were strangers to each other, but we were family. We spent the next several days trying to get to know each other. I learned one thing: Grandpa was not an easy man to figure out. He just didn't talk much. He seemed to be lost in his own far away thoughts. Sometimes I felt like there was an invisible wall between Grandpa and me. I had to figure out how to get the wall down. I figured the best thing I could do was try to make myself useful. The first few days I was with Grandpa, I didn't do much. I just sat in the house or walked around the yard getting used to things. I even let Grandpa fix our meals which were mighty plain. Grandpa would fix grits for breakfast; beans and cornbread for dinner; and offer me cornbread and sweet milk for later in the evening. No wonder Grandpa was so skinny.

Grandpa had a dog named Poker. Poker and me became real close fast. Poker and Grandpa were close too. One day, I was sitting on the stoop with Poker.

"Poker," I said, "how do I get close to Grandpa. I want Grandpa to love me and feel real glad I'm here."

Suddenly, out of the corner of my eye, I thought I saw Grandpa standing at the screen door. I hope he didn't hear me talking to Poker. When I turned around to look again, he was gone.

I had been at Grandpa's four days. I decided this was the day I was going to make myself useful. I was going to make Grandpa real glad I was here. I put back on the boy clothes and boots and decided I would clean Grandpa's house top to bottom. I started in the kitchen. I got me a warm sudsy bucket of water and just started in. Grandpa came in.

"What ya doing girl?" he asked.

"I'm scrubbing the kitchen," I answered.

He turned around and left without saying a word.

After about two hours of cleaning the kitchen, I got a fresh bucket of water and went on into the sitting room. I wiped down the walls and dusted all the furniture. While I was cleaning, I heard Grandpa in the kitchen whistling. I looked around the corner at Grandpa; he was mixing a bowl of cornbread and frying up some potatoes.

I went back to cleaning. After a while I heard Grandpa announce, "Dinner is on the table girl."

Evie

I washed up and joined Grandpa at the table. My mouth was sure watering. I guess I worked myself up quite an appetite. We had pinto bean, fried potatoes, cornbread, and sliced tomatoes. I can honestly say it was one of the best tasting meals I have ever had. I caught Grandpa looking at me, and if I wasn't mistaken, he had a little smile on his face. Maybe Grandpa was getting used to me being here after all.

After we finished our meal, I went back into the sitting room to finish cleaning.

Grandpa came in the room and said, "Don't kill yourself cleaning girl. We've got time on our side. You don't have to clean the place all in day."

"Ok Grandpa," I answered.

I finished what I was doing and then went outside to rinse my rags and the bucket out at the well. It was dusk with a faint breeze in the air. The air smelled fresh with a hint of autumn. It was a pretty late summer night. For the first time in a longtime I felt a feeling of happiness—not as happy as I was when Mama and Daddy were alive of course. I don't think I'll ever feel that happy again.

I walked into the house and found Grandpa setting up something in the sitting room. He had a little table in front of his chair. He was setting up to what looked to be a game.

"Have you ever played chess girl?" he asked.

"No, sir, I don't believe I have."

"Well, sit down here. I'll teach you. It's about time we did something besides work around here."

Grandpa spent hours that evening teaching me the game of chess.

"Come tomorrow night, you'll be able to challenge me in a game," Grandpa said.

"Grandpa, I think I'm ready to challenge you now."

"If you think you are ready, let's have at it," Grandpa said with a smile on his face.

Grandpa and me played for about an hour before I lost to him, He told me I gave him a run for his money. He leaned back in his chair; he seemed to be proud.

He said, "I can always tell how smart a man is by how he plays the game of chess. I don't mind saying I've got an awfully smart daughter." He quickly corrected himself and said, "I mean granddaughter."

Grandpa called me his daughter. I knew what I had to do right then and there. I had to tell him how I felt.

"Grandpa," I said, "I know I am your daughter, but in my heart, I am your granddaughter, and you are my grandpa. I just can't imagine anyone else being my Daddy except for the Daddy who raised me."

Grandpa looked at me long and hard and then said, "Well, child, I guess I can understand that. I guess Laura is your Mama and Sarah is your grandmother."

"Yes, sir. In my heart, that's how I think of things."

"Well, I guess daughter or granddaughter, either way, you're my girl. We won't worry about the details of things much. I guess I would like to let you know a thing or two about your birth mother. For this time, and this time only, I'm going to call her your mother. She was the one who gave you, life, child. I would like for you to know a few things about her. I would like to honor her in giving her child more knowledge of her."

"Yes, Grandpa, I would like very much to know more about her."

"She was a fine woman, the finest woman you could ever meet. Anyone who made her acquaintance loved her right off. She looked different than you and Laura. You both got blue eyes like my side of family. Sarah had green eyes, but not dull green eyes; they were pretty sparkling green eyes, like early spring grass covered with morning dew. They sparkled even brighter when she talked about Laura or the baby she was carrying, which was you. She had deep love for you even before you arrived."

I couldn't help the tears falling from my eyes as Grandpa was telling me about my birth mother. I suddenly felt sad that I never knew my very special birth mother. I felt a longing for the mother I never knew, but at the same time I felt a strong love and gratitude for the mother I did know. Grandpa handed me his handkerchief as he continued talking about my birth mother.

"She was very smart just like you. She could figure anything out; she always had hunches about things, and usually her hunches were right. She would say she had a feeling it was going to rain, and it wouldn't be any time at all that a rain cloud would be overhead and the heavens would pour out." Grandpa cleared his throat, wiped his eyes, and said, "Well, I just thought you should know a little about your mother. I mean grandmother."

"Thank you for telling me about my mother. It was very special to learn some things about her," I said as I gave Grandpa a hug.

Grandpa's eyes glistened. "You're welcome child. Sometimes the plans we have in life don't work out. God has something altogether different in mind. We just have to trust him and figure he knows best."

Grandpa stopped talking for a minute and looked like he was deep in his thinking. I got the feeling he was thinking about things that happened a long time ago.

After a while, Grandpa spoke up again. "Evelyn, since the day you were born, I loved you. Along with this love, I felt a burden. I had the burden of knowing I couldn't give you the care you were so deserving of. Laura came and lifted my burden and lifted her own burden by taking you has her own. As you probably know, she couldn't have any young'uns of her own. From time to time, I would feel I should have been the one raising you, but I felt peaceful knowing that you had a wonderful woman giving you all the love in the world."

Talking and thinking of Mama made Grandpa put his head in his hands and weep out loud.

"Grandpa we don't have to talk anymore," I said as I patted Grandpa on the back.

Grandpa raised his head up and said through teary eyes, "I just wish I would have had the chance to see you and Laura more often. She brought you back to see me when you were a wee little one. If I remember right, you were a little over a year old and you had just started walking. I was a fool back then. I wanted to ease my guilt. I started feeling Sarah would have been heartbroken if she knew I wasn't raising our daughter. I asked Laura if I could have you back. She got very upset. She asked me how I could ask such a thing. She said you belonged to her now. She never came around again. Once in a while, she would send me a picture. I haven't had one for many years though, not since you turned into a grown-up looking young lady."

"That explains it," I said quietly.

"Explains what?" Grandpa asked.

"It explains why Mama didn't speak of you much, except for at the end."

"You know, child, the Lord works in mysterious ways. He went and brought you back to me when I'm old and set in my ways. He is giving me another chance to raise you, to have you a part of my days."

Chapter 18

Grandpa and me needed to move forward. We tried not to speak of the sadness of missing our lost loved ones. Oh, every once in a while he would say something, or I would say something, but we would not let ourselves get sad. Move forward we did. My days were spent keeping house. I also took over the kitchen duties. Mama had taught me how to cook. I cooked a lot of things that Mama used to cook for Daddy and me. Grandpa liked to cook too, so sometimes we would cook together. I would tell him fun things about Mama, how she taught me this and that, how she had a lot of funny little sayings. Grandpa would smile and tell me he was sure glad Mama taught me how to make the best fried chicken, and chicken and dumplings, he ever had. I was going to put some meat on Grandpa's bones. I was already getting meat on my bones. The dress Miss Beth gave me was getting mighty tight. Grandpa seemed to notice too.

"Seems to me we need to go into town and get you some new clothes, child. You are about ready to break the seams of that dress."

The next morning, Grandpa took me into town in his old pickup that reminded me of Daddy's. We stopped at the dress shop in town. Both Grandpa and me had forgotten the warning that Brother John gave us about making sure I wasn't spotted. It seemed to be far from our minds.

At the shop, Grandpa handed me a twenty-dollar bill. It reminded me of when I had Mama's money. I felt a tinge of gilt; I should have protected Mama's money better. How unfair that a drunk ended up with Mama's hard saved money. Once again, I had to tell myself to move forward and not worry about the past. There was nothing I could do about it now.

I realized giving me the twenty dollars was a sacrifice for Grandpa. I would not spend it all, and I would spend it wisely, I reasoned to myself. I really did need another dress. Grandpa dropped me off at the dress shop while he went to the town market to get staples for our pantry.

I walked into the dress shop. The middle-aged clerk, who smelled of strong, rose-scented perfume greeted me. "Hello, young lady, may I help you find something today?"

"Yes, ma'am, I'm looking for a dress." As she gathered up several dresses for me to try on, she asked me several questions. She asked me my name. I told her who I was.

She quickly asked me if I was new to these parts because she had not heard of me before. I told her I was William Owens' granddaughter.

"Oh...I wasn't aware Mr. Owens had a granddaughter," she said, furrowing her brow. "I've lived in this town for years. I know a good bit about William. I had never heard he had a granddaughter." The nosey clerk seemed to be talking more to herself then to me.

I knew right away I was talking to the town gossip. I would need to be careful not to give her any more information. I had probably given her too much already. I wished Grandpa would have warned me. The woman continued to ask me questions. I pretended to be so busy looking for dresses that I didn't hear her. I quickly picked out two plain but pretty dresses. I gave the clerk my twenty-dollar bill. She gave me a little change back. I think she felt this was her chance to ask me more questions, but before she could ask another one, I darted out the door.

Whew! I was sure glad to be out of there.

I looked up the street to find Grandpa. As I was standing there, a truck full of boys drove by. They began hooting and hollering.

"Hey pretty girl! Where are you going?"

Suddenly, I felt Grandpa's arms around me.

"She is not going anywhere with you hoodlums! Get away from her!" he hollered.

I never had a boy notice me before; I didn't know quite how to feel about it. It made me feel real good that Grandpa looked out for me.

"Thank you, Grandpa," I said. "You need to be careful, girl. You are a pretty girl with a shape on you that boys like. We need to get you out of that tight dress into something that fits you better."

"Yes, sir. I think you will like the dresses I bought."

It was a quiet ride home. We were both thinking thoughts to ourselves. I was thinking how Mama always called me a late bloomer. She said she had been a late bloomer too. I guess I've bloomed. I sure look different in the mirror at the store. I looked like a grown woman. When we got home, I showed Grandpa the two dresses he bought me and thanked him again as I gave him back the change.

"Child, you should have spent the whole thing. I meant for you too."

"Thank you, Grandpa, but the two dresses are fine for now."

"You are a good girl. Laura raised you right—better than I could have done. I'm mighty grateful for that, God rest her sweet soul."

Chapter 19

Time went on. Our lives became a peaceful routine. I turned another year older living with Grandpa. I was now 16. Grandpa and I would work during the day. Some days, Grandpa insisted I do schoolwork. He got me books from the town library. I had not been to school since Daddy's death. After the day's work was done, Grandpa and I would play chess by the light of the kerosene lamp with Poker by our side. I was getting real good at chess. I would even beat Grandpa from time to time. I really liked playing chess: you had to think quick, and every move related to other moves. Grandpa said it was strategy. He would say, "Life is like chess. Making the right moves in life is important, and sometimes life requires using strategy."

After Grandpa and me played chess, I would lay awake every night and think about what Grandpa was teaching me. He seemed to be teaching me about life. He said that the world is made up of good and evil: the black pieces were evil, the while pieces were good. Of course, when Grandpa and I played, there was no good and evil; it was just us playing. We would mix it up. Sometimes I would be black and sometimes white. Towards the end of each game, it always took Grandpa and me longer to make moves because we had to spend time thinking. While Grandpa took his time, I would think about my life, about how I had good pawns and bad pawns in my life. I also had good and bad kings and queens, rooks, bishops, and knights. Mama and Daddy were the good queen and king. Evil Al was the evil king.

Finally, Grandpa moved his chess piece. Just as he moved his piece there was a loud pounding on the front door.

"Who in tarnation is that? No reason to be pounding so hard," Grandpa said with irritation in his voice.

I heard Grandpa arguing at the door. I walked over to find out what the problem was.

"Evelyn, go back into the kitchen!" Grandpa ordered.

The urgency in his voice made my heart skip a beat. They must have tracked me down! I ran back into the kitchen.

"I'm sorry, Bill, I have to take her in," I overheard the town's sheriff. "I got orders to place her under arrest. If I don't, I could be in a heap of trouble. They could come down here and arrest me for protecting a criminal."

"She didn't do nothing wrong, I tell you! It's all been a big misunderstanding!" Grandpa shouted.

"Well, fine then, she can explain herself to the law up there, but the fact is I have to take her in."

I knew by the way the sheriff was speaking that I would have to go with him, no matter what. I thought about running out the back door. I had already done that. I guess when it came right down to it, I was still running even now. I needed to stand up for myself. Mama always said truth rises to the top. I hoped she was right.

I grabbed up my few belongings and walked over to the door.

"It's ok, Grandpa, I'll go with him."

"No! Evelyn, I won't let you do that. I lost you once, I'm not going to lose you again," Grandpa said with tears in his eyes.

I wrapped my arms around him and promised him I would be back. Grandpa looked at the sheriff. His eyes had a pleading look in them.

As if to answer his look, the Sheriff said, "I'm sorry, Bill. This is just the way it has to be."

Grandpa's shoulders slumped. "Ok, but she won't be there long. You can bet my life on it."

The sheriff took me by the elbow.

"Wait!" Grandpa shouted, "I want you to take something with you."

Evie

Grandpa walked over to his chess board. He picked up the white queen and put it in my hands. "Here, my little queen. Remember, life is like a game of chess to be lived with great thought and strategy."

"Oh, Grandpa, I can't take the queen. Your chess set won't be complete."

"I want you to have it, Evelyn. When you hold it, I want you to have courage. I want you to remember all the things we talked about during all our hours playing chess. When you bring the chess piece back, my life will be complete because I'll have you in it again, where you belong."

I tucked the chess piece deep in my satchel. I hugged Grandpa hard and said, "Don't worry, Grandpa, I'll be back soon."

The sheriff led me out the door to the police car. He opened the door and said, "Ok, Missy, get in. Being that your Bill's kin, I won't handcuff you unless you give me a reason to. If you start showing signs of running off, I'll buckle those hands right up. Do you understand?"

"Yes, sir," I answered. I sure didn't want handcuffs on. It was bad enough having to ride down Main Street in the police car.

As we rode through town, it was as if everyone was expecting me. People were lined up along the road. Store owners and clerks were away from their stores watching us drive by. Of course, the middle-aged busybody from the dress shop was right out in front. I was tempted to wave, but I figured I better not. We pulled up to a little square building that said "JAIL" in big letters above the door. It looked to be the oldest building in town.

The sheriff grabbed my few belongings. I had left Mama's purse and all the important papers at Grandpa's for safekeeping. I could not risk anything happening to them. I'm sure glad I did, 'cause when we got to the jailhouse the sheriff started plundering through my bag. It was embarrassing! My under-panties and other personal things were in the bag.

He acted real business-like. "Sorry, missy, this is procedure. I have to make sure you don't have a weapon in here."

The sheriff escorted me into a tiny cell. He clanged the door shut and I was locked in. I felt like a caged animal, but as I looked around, I figured most animals had it better off than me. The tiny bed against the wall had a filthy mattress on it. It looked like the people who stayed here before me must have gotten sick. Also, it looked like many of them couldn't hold their bladders. How in heaven's name did the sheriff expect me to sleep on this filthy mattress?

"Sheriff?" I called out.

"Yeah?" he answered.

"The mattress on this bed is really dirty. Do you have anything to cover it?"

The sheriff looked at me like he didn't know whether to laugh or yell at me. He looked at the mattress.

"Yeah it is purty filthy, I guess. I'll see if I can dig up something to put on it."

He came back with two scratchy brown blankets. As he handed me the blanket, he said, "Here you go. I was just going to give you one of these to cover up with tonight, but seeing as the mattress is in the shape it's in, take another one. Use one to cover the mattress and one to cover yourself."

"Thank you kindly," I said.

I had nothing to do in the little cell except sit on the bed with the scratchy blanket under me. I sat wondering how people keep from going crazy when they have to spend years in jail. I sure wouldn't make a good prisoner. Suddenly, the sheriff came around the corner to the cell. He was holding a grey plate. The plate looked to have beans and a biscuit on it.

"Here you go Missy—dinner," the sheriff said.

"Thank you," I answered back.

Mama always taught me to have manners. "Please" and "thank you" were always appropriate. I figured it wouldn't hurt to use manners in here. I didn't figure the sheriff was used to people using their manners, cause when I said thank you, he looked bothered and mumbled something under his breath. I wondered if was saying, "You are welcome," but probably not.

The beans didn't look 'fitten to eat. They looked like they had been cooked a might too long. The biscuits could have broken my tooth right out had I decided to bite right down on it. Instead, I left it in my mouth for a few seconds and let it soften a little. The beans were dry and didn't have much flavor. I figured I'd better go ahead and try to eat them. I didn't know when I'd be able to eat again. I got a few bites down but that's all I could muster.

The sheriff came back about a half hour later. He picked up my plate and said, "I guess you ain't too hungry, are ya, Missy."

"I guess not," I answered, but truth was I was mighty hungry. I just couldn't eat that mess.

I guess the little bit I did eat didn't sit well with me at all. A few hours into the night, my belly took to growling something fierce. Then I needed to relieve myself bad.

"Sheriff!" I yelled. He didn't come,

Oh my! I felt if he didn't come and let me go to the toilet soon, I might just mess myself.

"Sherriff!" I called urgently.

"Yeah, what cha wanting?" the sheriff answered as he stumbled to my cell rubbing his eyes. I guess I woke him up from deep sleep.

"So sorry to wake you, sir, but I have to use the toilet!"

He mumbled something. I think he was swearing under his breath. He unlocked my cell, "You better not be trying something, Missy. I can still use those cuffs on you."

"No sir, I really have to go," I said, feeling real desperate. My stomach growled real loud, and I doubled over with pain. I guess he now believed me because he picked me up and carried me right outside to the outhouse.

"There you go, Missy, do your business. I'll be right outside your door."

When I first sat down on the cold wood seat, I thought I'd be able to relieve myself right away, but instead I was gripped with a horrible stomach cramp.

"Ooow," I moaned.

The sheriff was outside the door. "You ok, Missy? Are you having woman troubles or something?"

"No, the beans you gave cramped my belly," I answered.

Finally, after several minutes, relief came. My body rid itself of those nasty beans and everything else I had eaten in a week's time. I sat there a good long time. I couldn't worry about the sheriff on the other side of the door. A few times, I would stand up after I'd wiped myself, but I'd feel the urge to go again. I was grateful there was some old newsprint to wipe myself with. If I would have had nothing, I would have been in a real fix.

I heard the sheriff purposely clear his throat. I forgot that he had been waiting for me. I quickly slid off the old wood seat.

"Ow!" I felt something painful go right into the left side of my fanny. I bet I got a splinter. The outhouse was old and had not been kept up. Daddy always took good care of our outside toilet. He would sand and paint the seat a couple of times a year. Oh well. I'd have to deal with the splinter later. Hopefully, it wasn't too big. How I would even get it out myself, I just didn't know.

I opened the latch to the outhouse.

"Feeling better?" the sheriff asked.

"Yes, sir, I just didn't take to those beans."

The sheriff looked a little troubled and said, "Yeah, I bet Matthew, my boy, brought you the wrong food. I bet he brought you the beans and bread meant for the slop bucket."

That news made my stomach wrench in another way. I ran a few feet from the path to the outhouse and puked. The sheriff took a handkerchief from his pocket.

"Here you go," he said. I wiped my mouth on it. The handkerchief felt a little crusty, like he had used it many times. This made me puke again.

"Wait right here. I'll get some water," the sheriff said, looking a little sorry for me. "Don't go running off though."

My whole body was shuddering. I figured this day would be in my memory as one of the most miserable of my life. Of course, there were a few worse days, but I couldn't let my mind think on those things right now. The sheriff brought a clean wet cloth and a cup of water to me. He started to say something about the beans. I held up my hand, letting him know not to continue talking.

"Oh, I guess I better not talk about the be...yeah, well, ok. Let's go back in."

I felt weak as I walked back into the cell. I was trembling. I guess the sheriff felt sorry for me 'cause he went and got me another blanket. I heard him talking on the phone with someone. I figured it was his wife. He was telling her everything. I had to cover my ears during some parts of his conversation to keep from feeling sick again.

Shortly after the sheriff had talked on the phone, I heard a woman's voice. "Where is she, Maxwell? I just can't even imagine what that poor child must be going through right now."

"I told you: she's locked up in the cell. She is a prisoner you know."

I looked up to see a lady. She was a pleasant-looking, middle-aged lady with a sweet, caring smile. "You poor dear! I am so sorry about what you were given for dinner."

I willed myself not to think about what she was saying for fear of getting sick again.

The nice lady went on to say "I brought you some fresh dinner if you would like; it's beef stew and corn bread. This is what you were supposed to have been served."

"Thank you," I said softly. I leaned up on the bed. As I did, I felt a burning pain on my back hip.

"Ow!" I said out loud, feeling the splinter.

The sheriff's wife must have noticed me wincing with pain.

"Are you alright, dear?" she asked.

I knew this was my chance. I needed help with my blister and this kind motherly lady could help me.

"It seems I got a blister from the outhouse," I explained.

"Oh my," she uttered. She quickly took charge. She told the sheriff not to come back to cell until she said so, and she meant it. The sheriff said ok but asked why. She told him it was none of his concern. I could tell who wore the britches in this family, as Daddy would say.

"Now lean over. Let's take a look. Don't be bashful! I have three daughters: one is still at home; the other two went and got married. Then we had our little surprise, Matthew. He was the one who brought you the bad food. He is our special child. You have to watch him sometimes—he doesn't always think the way we do. Oh, here I am going on and on and I haven't even told you my name yet. My name is Gladys. My daddy wanted to name me Gladiola, but my Mama didn't like the sound of that."

Miss Gladys sure liked to talk, I thought to myself. I smiled as she went on and on about anything and everything. I pushed my embarrassment aside and pulled down my underpanties and turned with my back side facing Gladys.

"Oh honey! Yes! You sure do have a splinter and it's a doozy. It looks to be about two inches long. I'm going to have to fetch some things from the house. I'll need some rubbing alcohol, a needle, and tweezers. While I'm gone, you just go ahead and eat some decent dinner."

Gladys left my cell shaking her head. I heard her scolding her husband for not having an outside toilet fittin' to sit on. She told him he should be ashamed of himself. I couldn't help but smile to myself. I felt very grateful for

Gladys. I felt grateful the Lord had sent someone to take my splinter out. Lord only knows what would have happened if she would not have come along.

I took one look at the fresh food Gladys brought me. I couldn't help feeling sick just looking at the food. I nibbled a little on the cornbread, but that was all I could muster.

Soon, Gladys was back. It seemed it was no-time at all and the two-inch splinter was out of my backside. There was a look of pride on her face as she pulled the splinter out. She looked as though she had a caught a prized fish.

"Thank you so much, Miss Gladys. It feels much better."

"I'm not finished quit yet," she said. She took the alcohol and rubbed it over my flesh. It burned something fierce.

"That's to keep any infection from setting up. You sure have a nasty piece of wood in your bottom. We need to do everything we can to help you heal as good as new."

I smiled in gratitude. Miss Gladys gave me a hug. She reminded me off Miss Opal, the way her plump arm brought me into her chest.

I felt that seeing my backside made Miss Gladys feel the need to mother me. She said she was going to send her son over with a softer pillow and blanket. Before Gladys left, she wanted to know what happened to put me in this predicament.

Before I could answer her, the sheriff said, "Now Gladys, you know you are not supposed to ask law question to the prisoners."

"Oh hush, Maxwell. I just know this girl didn't do anything wrong. I feel she is innocent."

"Well, then, they will find that out in Illinois. It's not our concern. Our job is to get her from here to there. Right now, she needs to get some sleep," the sheriff said as he turned out the lights and lead Gladys away from the cell.

"I'll send Matthew over with a soft blanket and pillow," she said over her shoulder. I looked at Gladys and mouthed the words "I'm innocent" to her.

She mouthed back, "I know."

After they left, I heard the sheriff say, "Now Gladys, we are not running a hotel here. We can't give prisoners special treatment."

I heard Gladys argue with him, but I could not make out what she said. I squirmed on the scratching blanket, relieved a softer blanket was coming.

A few minutes later, I heard Miss Gladys again: "Now, Maxwell, you see to it that girl gets this soft blanket and pillow.

Those scratchy blankets might work ok for ruff-skinned no-gooders, but they will rub that girl's skin raw."

She went on to say, "And you make sure someone decent comes to pick up that girl. Just imagine if she were our daughter. She is a pretty girl. We don't want anybody looking at her the wrong way."

"I know, don't worry, I'll make sure. Why don't you get on home now. I'll be wanting some dinner before too long."

I smiled to myself and thanked the Lord for putting another nice piece in my life game of chess.

The soft blanket and pillow felt like heaven next to my skin; I fell to sleep right away.

I woke up with a jolt to the sound of male voices. I noticed someone had put a basin of water next to me. I quickly splashed my face and brushed through my hair with my fingers.

The sheriff unlocked my cell and said, "Ok, Missy, go ahead and attend to any private business because you are going to be hitting the road soon. A deputy sheriff will be escorting you back up to Peoria, Illinois. You'll be traveling a good many hours."

I gathered my few belongings and headed out back to relieve myself. The sheriff must have trusted that I wouldn't run off because he didn't follow me this time. Thankfully, this visit to the outhouse was a lot better than the last. I changed into fresh panties. I wanted a bath, but a bath would have to wait. I did the best I could with the basin of water in the cell.

As I walked back into the jailhouse, I dreaded seeing who I was going to be forced to spend hours with on the trip to Peoria. I braced myself for an old, rough sheriff, but the sheriff wasn't old or rough at all; he was young. I'm not good at guessing age, but I didn't figure he was much older than me. He looked at me. His eyes traveled from my face to my feet to my feet and back to my face. I was wearing one of my new dresses that Grandpa had bought me. I would have worn my britches, but they didn't fit me anymore. The young deputy realized he was staring at me, and he knew I knew it. His face turned red as a ripe tomato. He was fair in his complexion, so it was easy to tell when he was embarrassed. He seemed a little nervous too.

The deputy and the sheriff walked me out the door. I was surprised to see many of the townspeople gathered around the jailhouse. Grandpa was there too. He walked over to me, gave me a hug, and said, "We'll get out of this trouble, Evelyn. I promise you we will."

"I know, Grandpa," I answered, not wanting him to let me go.

165

Gladys came over and hugged me too. There were several women standing next to her. They looked a lot like her. I figured they were her daughters. All these people standing around were wishing me luck, even people I didn't know. I wasn't quite sure why. I don't know if it was because I was kin to Grandpa, or because the sheriff's wife took a liking to me and spread it around town that I was innocent. Whatever the reason, it touched me. I felt tears fill my eyes. I quickly looked away. I didn't want Grandpa to think I was sad; I was touched by the care these people were showing me. The way I looked at it, God was giving me more pieces in my chess game of life.

The young deputy opened the back door of the police car and guided me in. I was a prisoner; I needed to sit in the back seat while being taken back to Peoria. I wanted to yell out that I shouldn't be a prisoner and had done nothing wrong, but I held my tongue, knowing it wouldn't do any good. It was comforting to know that many of the town's people believed in my innocence, but these people were not the judge and jury in Peoria.

Chapter 20

We were now driving down the road. We had about twelve hours to go. An hour and one half went by and the young deputy didn't utter a word to me. Every once in a while, I noticed him looking in the rearview mirror at me. I was beginning to wonder if we would be spending the entire trip in silence when he finally spoke up.

"Name's Josh. Well, it's actually Joshua, but people that know me call me Josh."

I smiled and nodded.

He began again. "I just thought maybe you needed to know my name."

There was a long pause and then he said, "Just in case you needed something."

Another pause.

"Course, you could just call me deputy."

I could tell the young deputy was embarrassed because the back of his neck turned red.

I felt I needed to say something to calm his nerves. "Thank you for telling me your name, Joshua."

"Well, make sure to let me know if you need anything. And you can go ahead and call me Josh."

We continued down the road in awkward silence. Finally, Josh cleared his throat and asked if I was hungry. Being that I got sick the day before and was only able to eat a little of Gladys's cornbread, I was hungry. I didn't have much nourishment in me.

"Yes, I do feel a bit hungry," I answered.

"Ok, there is a little café up the road a piece. We could stop and have a midday meal if you would like?"

"I'd like that."

We pulled up to a little cafe. My stomach began growling. Yes, I was hungry.

Josh looked nervous. "Usually, I have to handcuff myself to the prisoner when we go to a public place, but I don't see a need to do that to you."

"Thank you," I said simply. We walked side by side into the café. We got a few curious stares considering we did get out of a police car and all. We sat at a corner table.

The waitress came over and said, "Hey there, officer. What can I get for you and the missus today?"

Evie

The missus. The waitress described me as the missus. She must think the police deputy and I were married. The thought of that made my face grow hot. Grandpa did say that I was near courting age. My next birthday was in a few months. I would be seventeen. I wasn't thinking about courting though; I had to get myself out of trouble. This lawman wouldn't think too kindly on courting a prisoner.

We both ordered the special of the day: roast beef and potatoes with green beans on the side.

"I don't know about you, but I'm mighty hungry," Josh said. It seemed he was trying hard to think of something to say.

"I'm feeling a little hungry myself," I said. My saying seemed to take away some of Josh's nervousness because he started talking to me.

"Hope you don't mind me saying so, but you don't look like a girl that would be in this kind of trouble."

"Thank you," I said simply.

We sat in silence waiting for our food. Joshua seemed to be building up the courage to ask me more questions. Finally, he asked, "How did you get yourself into all this trouble anyway?"

I answered him quickly by saying, "First of all, I did not get myself into all this trouble. Trouble came to me. I did not welcome it, that's for sure." We sat in silence again. After a few minutes went by, I asked him, "Do you really want to know?"

"I do," he answered, looking me square in the eyes. His handsome face and pretty blue eyes looked right into mine.

I felt a little flutter in my tummy. "Ok," I said. "I will start from the beginning."

I started with Daddy's death. If I wasn't mistaken, I'd swear his eyes had tears in them. Then I began telling him everything. It kind of reminded me of when I told Brother John and Miss Beth everything. I trusted them and I felt I could trust Josh the deputy. There is a feeling that comes over a person when they know they can trust someone. There is also a feeling that comes over a person when they feel that they can't trust someone. That's exactly the feeling I got from Evil Al, right off.

When our food came, we quit talking and just ate. We were both hungry, and the food tasted very good. Josh cleaned his plate and finished off the little bit I left on my plate. We left the café and walked back to the police car.

Josh said, "Heck, I don't see no reason why you have to sit in the back. How about you just ride in the front seat? Of course, you'll have to return to the back seat before we drive into Peoria."

"I don't mind sitting in the back seat," I said.

"I know," he said, "but I want to hear more of your story. I have to strain to hear you, you sitting in the back and all."

"Oh alright," I said as I climbed into the front seat. I hid a smile, wondering if Josh had other motives for wanting me to sit next to him.

As we traveled down the road, there was silence until Josh asked me to continue my tale. He seemed really eager to know. I guess I had stopped talking at an interesting part: where Al Jenkins started courting Mama and I didn't like it. I continued with my life story; sometimes Josh would stop me and ask me for more details. I would tell him the best I could remember. Sometimes Josh would shake his head, like he couldn't believe what I was telling him, only I knew he believed me. Sometimes he would just say, "Lord have mercy."

I talked and talked for what seemed like hours. Finally, I caught up to today. Josh pulled the police car over, which surprised me.

"What's wrong?" I asked. I wondered what in the world he was doing.

We sat alongside the road. Josh looked at me for a good long minute and said, "Evie, I sure am sorry. I know as sure as I'm breathing that every word of what you are telling me is true. I'm going to do everything I can to keep you out of prison and help you get your name cleared."

Sitting there next to Josh, him believing me and wanting to help me and all, I couldn't help myself: I took hold of his hand with both my hands and said, "Thank you so much Joshua." I did it without thinking, but when our hands touched something mighty powerful happened. I think Josh felt if too, cause his neck got all red around the collar and his hands started shaking a little.

I pulled my hands away from his. Josh cleared his throat and said, "I guess we best be on our way."

The rest of the trip was spent with me asking Josh questions. I figured it wasn't fair for him to know all about me and for me to know nothing about him. I found out that he was born and raised in Peoria. He had two brothers and a sister. His mama and daddy were still living. He came from a long line of lawmen. His grandpa was a bounty hunter his dad was a sheriff for years and had recently become governor of the state. His older brother was a lawyer. His mama used to be a schoolteacher but now she stayed on and took care of his grandmother. Josh seemed excited talking about his family. I could tell he loved them very much. It warmed my heart to hear about them. It made me miss my own family very much.

Chapter 21

We were about two hours from Peoria. It seemed Josh was taking his time getting there. We stopped for dinner, only this time it wasn't a café: it was a nice restaurant with nice, snowy-white napkins and shiny silverware and glasses that were called goblets. I had never been to a place like that before I didn't know what to order. I let Josh order for me. He ordered steak for both of us. If I didn't know better, I would say that Josh was trying to court me. He even pulled my chair out for me to sit on. We enjoyed our meal. We laughed and talked and had a good time.

At the end of our meal, Josh got real quiet. "I sure hate it that you have to stay in that Peoria Jail, Evie. You are just too sweet and too pretty to spend time in jail, but mark my words you won't be there long."

"I sure hope not," I said quietly.

I left the restaurant with a heavy heart, knowing what lay ahead. I said a silent prayer that I would be able to handle being in another jailhouse. I expected to drive right to the

Peoria jail, but instead Josh pulled in alongside the graveyard on the edge of town.

"Evie, we need to talk a bit before we drive into town."

"Alright," I said.

"I know we haven't known each other very long, but we have had hours of conversation during this trip. I was thinking it would take a lot of courting to add up to all these hours we spent together. What I'm getting at is that I like you, Evie. I like you a whole lot."

He then took my hand and said, "I would like your permission to court you after this whole thing is straightened out."

I looked at Josh. I felt stunned. So many thoughts were going through my mind. I wasn't even sure I knew how to court. I did know Joshua Harrison was the kindest boy I had ever met. My stomach did a lot of fluttering when I was around him. It took me a while to answer Josh. I think this made him feel foolish because he started rambling on about how he was sorry, and how he hoped he hadn't made me feel uncomfortable.

I decided I needed to put him out of his misery and answer him.

Evie

"No, Josh, you did not make me uncomfortable, and yes I would like very much to court you when I'm out of all this trouble."

Josh then lit up like a sky full of lightning. He grabbed me and hugged me tight. Then he kissed me on my cheek. I didn't mind one bit—truth be told, I was hoping he would kiss me flat on the mouth. My face grew hot just thinking of how his lips would feel on mine. I was satisfied with just hoping someday I would feel his lips on mine.

"Ok, Miss Evie, let's get going! The sooner we get there, the sooner we can get you out of jail and the sooner I can court you."

We got into town. It all looked so familiar yet different. Then I suddenly realized the town wasn't different, I was different. I had grown up a lot in the last few years since Daddy's death. I was fourteen when Daddy died. Now, I was about to turn seventeen. I was jarred from my thoughts when Josh took me by the elbow and guided me into the jail.

I didn't recognize this sheriff. He must have come on during the time I was away. He was much different than Sheriff Harrington.

"Well, well," the sheriff said, "You finally showed up with the prisoner. I expected you to pull up a couple of hours ago."

175

Josh did not give the sheriff an explanation. He simply guided me into the jailhouse.

The sheriff took a piece of paper from Josh's hand. "Ok, I'll take over from here."

"I can put her in the cell," Josh offered.

The sheriff shrugged. "Alright." He handed Josh the keys. "Here you go. Lock her up while I go file these papers."

We both walked into the cramped cell.

"Evie," Josh said with pain in his eyes. "I hate leaving you here, you don't belong. I lock up boozers and thieves, not sweet innocent girls like you."

Our eyes locked. I seemed to be having a hard time catching my breath, and my eyes were tearing up. I felt emotional because of my feelings for Josh and the dread of having to be in jail again. He must have read my mind because he gently took his hands and put my hair behind my ears then with his thumb. He gently wiped the tears from my cheeks while whispering, "Don't worry, you'll be out of here soon."

The sheriff shouted from his desk. "Hey! How long does it take to lock up a prisoner?"

Josh gave me a little rub on my upper arm and left the cell. Reluctantly, he locked the door. Then he went back front and gave the keys to the sheriff.

I soon heard arguing.

Evie

"What! Are you crazy, kid? You're getting all lovestruck for a prisoner! You go home and tell your mama and daddy this and they'll have your hide—and mine too! You might not realize this, but the sweet little girl of yours is in here with murder charges, and just one but two. Sometimes those sweet little things can fool you. They look all innocent on the outside, but they are as mean as snakes on the inside."

"She is not like that! She is innocent and I'm going to prove it," Josh said with a strained voice.

"That little trip from there to here really gotcha didn't it? You seem to be thinking with that thing between your legs instead of your brain."

Josh looked angry and took a step towards him.

"Don't you even think about it," I heard the sheriff shout.

I saw Josh stop right in front of the sheriff.

"Josh, please don't hit the sheriff," I pleaded under my breath. Josh turned away from the sheriff and stormed out of the jailhouse.

"Whew!" I sighed with relief.

Josh would have been in so much trouble if he would have hit the sheriff. He would have probably lost his job and got arrested all because of me.

"Thank you, Joshua, for taking up for me and thank you for not getting yourself into a whole heap of trouble," I said out loud to Josh, even though he wasn't there.

Chapter 22

I sat down in the chair next to my bed. I felt glad this cell wasn't as filthy as the one in Tennessee. The sheriff came back to my cell with clothes. "Here, Miss, you need to put these prison clothes on. Leave your civilian clothes on the table. I'll pick them up in a few minutes."

He walked away.

"Surely you don't expect me to undress in this cell, sir!" I yelled after him.

The sheriff looked uncomfortable but seemed to realize that it would not be right for me to undress in the open cell.

"Hmph. We don't usually have female prisoners. I haven't run into this problem before. Well…I'll see if I can find something to hang on the cell bars to give you some privacy." He came back with a blanket and rope. He gathered up two corners of the blanket and tied them to the cell bars. "There you go. You'll have privacy behind this blanket. Just pull it down when you are done."

After the sheriff walked away, I slowly unfolded the garment and dust flew everywhere. The garment was the ugliest dress I'd ever seen. It was a plain grey cotton shift that smelled old and musty. How was I supposed to put this awful thing against my skin? Knowing I didn't have a choice, I removed my clothes and put the ugly dress on—if you could call it a dress. It looked more like a big tent. Then I folded my clothes and put them on the table, just as the sheriff had ordered. I untied the rope and yanked the blanket down, although I wish I could have left it up; it seemed less like jail cell with the blanket up. The sheriff came back to my cell and gathered up my clothes. He looked at me and grunted, handing me one of the ropes he used to tie up the blanket.

"Here; it looks like you could use this to tie around your waist. I guess the women prisoners we had before you had more meat on their bones than you do."

"Thank you," I said as I tied the rope around my waist. At least now it was not dragging on the ground.

I sat down on the chair in my cell, not knowing what to expect next. I noticed an old Bible on the table. I picked it up and the pages fell open to Psalm 46:1. I read the scripture: *God is our refuge and strength, a very present help in trouble.*

Thank you, God, for being my refuge and my strength. I really need you now in my time of trouble.

Evie

At about 9:45 p.m., the sheriff allowed me to use the bathroom. I was very grateful for the indoor plumbing. He said I should take care of my business before he called "Lights out" at ten o'clock. He said it was standard procedure that all prisoners need to be retired for the night at ten.

I laid down on the cot in the stuffy cell and tried to fall asleep. I felt uncomfortable and hot in the big tent dress. I wish I could have taken it outside and shaken it because it smelled musty. After tossing and turning for many hours, I finally fell asleep. I had a terrible nightmare: I kept seeing evil Al. He was laughing and saying, "I got you now!"

My nightmare must have spilled over into real life because when I opened my eyes there he was!

He was right there, looking through the cell bars, staring right at me with his evil, narrow eyes. At first, I thought I was seeing things. I kept blinking, but he didn't go away. I sat up in bed, shuddering at the apparition before me.

"Thought you got away did you, filthy child?" Evil Al sneered.

I heard myself gasp. "How did you get in here?"

"Ha! Ha! Scared you, did I?" he laughed.

"You aren't going to get away with this!" I spat, with as much hate as I could muster.

He laughed again. "Not going to get away with this? Let me assure you, naïve girl, I already have gotten away with it. The way I see it, I've gotten away with many things. Let's see: I have a nice home and property, compliments of your poor deceased mother. I don't recall paying one dime for anything! It's too bad my daughter is a murderer and can't enjoy life with me. She'll be busy spending the rest of her life in prison. Ha! Ha!"

"I would rather spend the rest of my life in jail then spend two minutes with you," I answered.

Still laughing, he turned on his heels and left.

I was tempted to yell at Evil Al, "You are wrong! You'll soon be the one behind these bars!"

But then I thought of my chess games with Grandpa. Grandpa taught me that sometimes you just have to hold your tongue and not give anything away. Jump on them when they least expect it.

I would let Evil Al think he had won, but in the end, he would get what's coming to him.

That afternoon, Josh came to my cell. He had a very sad look on his face.

"I don't like seeing you here, Evie," he said. "You just don't belong in a place like this. You shouldn't be made to wear a thing like that either."

"I'll get out of here soon, Josh. Somehow, someway."

Josh smiled. His eyes brightened with some hope. He told me his next bit of news.

"Evie, I've been talking to my brother, Steven. You know, the lawyer. He practices in Chicago, but he said he would be happy to help. He told me to get all the information I could from you. He wants to know all about the day you discovered the Smiths dead."

"Josh, I already told you about it," I reminded him, dreading the thought of having to tell it again.

"I know, and I'm sure sorry to ask you to relive it again, but I need to write it down this time."

Josh sat beside me as I laid down on the cell bed. I closed my eyes and began recalling the events of that awful day. Josh got his pen and paper ready and motioned for me to begin. So, I did…

"I remember I slept in my clothes the night before because I wanted to be able to leave real quick-like. I kept Mama's purse in my dress pocket. I had fallen asleep. Next thing I knew, Al Jenkins was laying down beside me in my bed. It scared me to death to see him there. He told me not to be afraid. He said he wanted to make up for all the pain he had caused me. He said I could either accept his apology or I could meet up with Mama and Daddy in heaven. He said Leonard and his 'fat wife' would be joining them soon. I wondered why he was telling me this. I remember worrying about the Smiths. He looked so evil and scary. I feared what he would do to them and what he was going to do to me. He tried to kiss me. He, he put his—"

I gagged at the memory of Evil Al putting his tongue in my mouth. It was almost unbearable to think about.

Josh looked at me with sympathy in his eyes. "It's ok, Evie, I wrote enough stuff down for today. We can start over again tomorrow."

"No," I said, thinking about some of the advice Grandpa gave me while playing chess. A person has got to stick to their game. Interrupting breaks the train of thought, which could cost them their game.

"I want to continue," I explained to Josh.

"Are you sure, Evie? We don't have to continue."

"Yes. I feel it would be best if we just keep going."

Josh flipped the page of his notebook pen in hand ready to take more notes.

I paused for a minute then I went on explaining what happened after that horrible kiss.

"I actually threw up after he kissed me. He put his tongue in my mouth—I had never heard of such a thing! His tongue was like a big, fat, stinky snake slithering in where it didn't belong." I shuddered at the memory. "I threw up in his mouth. Al Jenkins spit and called me a sickening little tramp. He yelled, 'Get ready to see your Mama and Daddy!' He raised his hand to hit me, but I was quicker than he was. I grabbed the hammer I had hidden under my pillow and cracked him on the head with it. He fell on top of me! Al Jenkins isn't a big man, but it felt like he weighed five hundred pounds! I pulled with all my strength to get out from under him. Finally, I got free. I made sure Mama's purse was still deep in my pocket and took off running as fast as I could. I ran as fast as I could to Leonard and Olive's house. I needed to warn them about Al Jenkins.

"I was so scared! I pounded and pounded on the door, but they didn't come, so I turned the knob and went on in. I yelled for them. It smelled like gas. I walked over to the stove. Every burner was turned on. I ran towards the Smith's bedroom I almost tripped on Skipper their dog. Skipper was dead!"

I found myself tearing up. I held up one finger to Josh. I had to take a little break before I could go on talking. It still made me so sad to think of Skipper. He was such a friendly dog. He probably greeted his killer with a welcome lick on the hand, like he did everyone else.

Josh understood I needed a break. He put his pen and paper down and started talking about other things. He talked about having to round up some petty thieves in town. I asked him what they stole. He laughed and said, "Shirts and under drawers off Miss. Blackwell's clothesline."

I laughed too. Josh went on tell to tell me his brother would be coming in a few days, and he would give him all the notes he had taken. I told him that I sure appreciated his brother helping me. I said I prayed God would help me line up all my pieces.

"All your pieces?" Josh asked.

I explained to him how Grandpa used the game of chess to teach me about life.

"Josh, your brother Steven is one of my most important game pieces. He is going to help get me out of trouble, and for this I am grateful."

Josh smiled his handsome smile. "Evie, you are the most interesting girl I have ever met." He laughed. "I'd like to think that I could be privileged enough to be one of your game pieces someday."

Before I could answer him, the sheriff came back to the cell.

"I thought you was just getting a statement from the prisoner. Looks to me like you are getting more than that. It appears there is a little courting going on here."

Josh's face and neck turned red. It was sure obvious to me Josh and sheriff didn't take too kindly to each other.

"I'm writing down statements as you can see," Josh answered in an irritated voice.

The sheriff glanced at Josh's notes, grunted, and walked away.

Josh had talked about the sheriff on our trip here. He said the sheriff resented him and thought the only reason Josh got hired was because his daddy was a hot shot lawman. I was beginning to think Josh's hunch was right. Josh also told me that the sheriff gave him all the jobs he didn't want to do. The sheriff did not want to escort the prisoner from Peoria, so he ordered Josh to do it. Josh said it turned out to be the best job he was ever given. Then he winked at me and smiled that handsome smile of his.

After the sheriff interrupted Josh and me, he ordered Josh to go to the tavern down the street and stop some ruckus that was going on. Josh knew he had to follow orders, so he reluctantly went out the door down to the tavern.

Before he left, he came back to my cell and said, "I'm sorry, Evie. I've got to go take care of this, but I will be back."

He turned to leave, then came back and said, "I'm going to see about bringing you some decent dinner."

"Thank you, Josh, and please be careful," I said before he left.

He smiled shyly, as if it touched him, and said, "I will."

I had to admit that I really was beginning to care for Josh. I could not bear the thought of something happening to my new friend, my only friend here. If I were honest with myself, I would have to say he was becoming more than a friend. My heart sure fluttered around him; all he had to do was look at me with those pretty blue eyes and I would lose myself in thoughts of him.

Josh returned that evening with two covered plates.

"No eating with the prisoners," the ornery sheriff said.

"It's ok, Dullie, it really is," Josh said, with sternness in his voice.

"I guess you checked with that daddy of yours and got an ok even though it doesn't go along with the rules."

"Dullie, nowhere in the law books does it say that a lawman can't eat with a prisoner," Josh protested.

Josh came back to my cell chuckling. He admitted he didn't know for sure what the law books said about eating with prisoners, but he was pretty sure Dullie didn't know either.

He sat the plates down on the bedside table and uncovered them. It was roast beef smothered with gravy, potatoes, carrots, and a dinner roll.

Evie

"Josh, thank you so much! The food looks delicious, and the plates are lovely. Which diner in town serves food on plates like these?"

"That would be my Mama's kitchen. Actually, these used to be my grandmother's plates, but when she died, Mama got them."

"Oh, Josh, you didn't have to bring me food on your mother's inherited fine china."

"Pretty china for a pretty girl," Josh said sweetly.

"Ughh!" came from the front of the jailhouse. "Dullie, don't you have anything to do besides eavesdrop?"

"I'm going to find something to do to keep from hearing you two lovebirds, or should I say jailbirds?" the sheriff shouted back.

Joshua and I talked all through our delicious meal. "I told Mama about you. I hope you don't mind. I just felt the need to tell somebody, and Mama is the listening type. I swear I saw tears in her in her eyes by the time I was finished talking. Anyway, she said she wanted to make you a good dinner."

When Josh was talking about his mama, it made me remember my mama. I looked away with tears in my eyes.

"Oh, Evie, I'm sure sorry. I didn't mean to make you cry. I should have asked your permission to talk to Mama about you."

189

"No, Josh. It was just fine that you told your mama about me. It's just that sometimes I start missing my mama and I was thinking how much I wished I could tell her about you. I wish I could tell her about a lot of things. I'm missing out on her and she is missing out on me."

Josh held me in his arms and did the sweetest thing: he kissed each one of my tears away. He then kissed me gently on the lips—not a kiss that some boys take from girls, but a kiss that said everything would be okay.

Josh held me close and whispered, "Everything will work out. You'll see."

I found myself thinking again of why I didn't have Mama. It was because of Evil Al. I felt more determined than ever to get out of jail. I needed to prove my innocence and somehow show the world who the real criminal was.

"Josh, do you have that tablet of paper with you? I'm ready to have you continue writing what I remember about that day. Let's see…where did I leave off?" Joshua reached into a little case and pulled out the writing tablet. "Well, Evie, you left off at a sad place. It was when you found the Smiths dead."

"Oh yes, now I remember. Well, I might as well get it over with."

Once again, I began recalling that dreadful day. I remembered thinking how strange it was that Skipper didn't bark. He always barked when someone walked up to the house. I thought he was sleeping, but when I bent down to pet him he was already cold to the touch. Then it struck me the gas that escaped from the stove had put poison in the air. I ran into the Smith's bedroom and yelled for them to get up. But it was too late; they were dead too. They died in their sleep, not even knowing what killed them. I remember hearing myself scream.

The next thing I remember is seeing headlights shining through the picture window. I looked out the window. It was Evil Al in Daddy's truck. Remembering it made me shake just like the night I was there. Josh saw me shaking. He put a blanket around my shoulders.

"Thank you," I said, continuing with my story. "I knew I had to get out of there. Evil Al was coming after me, and Lord only knew what he would do to me after crashing the hammer down on his head. My heart never beat so hard and fast in all my life. I ran out the back door across the yard and behind the shed.

"I hid behind the shed. I didn't dare move a muscle. I peeked around the shed and saw Evil Al coming out the back door carrying a lantern. I had to get away before him before he cornered me and worked more of his evil. Behind the shed was a thick wooded area. I remember having to jump over barbed wire. The good Lord was looking out for me; I didn't get hurt at all. I figured Evil Al heard me, and probably saw me, so I took off like a jackrabbit. I ran as fast as my legs could take me. I thought I heard shots from a gun off in the distance, so I started running zig-zag. I felt like a hunted animal. The sky was really dark that night, which was a good thing and a bad thing. It was good because Evil Al couldn't see me, but it was bad because I kept tripping. I'd get right back up and start running again."

Josh shook his head and said, "Boy it makes my legs ache just thinking about how much you must have run that night. I'm sure glad you got away, Evie. I can't stand the thought of what that man might have done to you if he would have caught you."

"Thank you, Josh," I said.

I was starting to feel tired. I guess all the remembering got the best of me. Josh gathered up the plates and told me to get some rest.

"Joshua," I said. "Please thank your Mama for me. The dinner was really delicious. I know I didn't eat it all; I guess my appetite won't be back to normal until I get out of here."

"That's ok, Evie. I should know better than to fill a small girl's plate so full," Josh said, smiling. He hugged me again, only this time he also kissed me sweetly on the forehead.

"I'll try to be back in the morning," he said.

Evie

Josh walked away, and then turned around as if he suddenly remembered something. "My brother Steven will be here the day after tomorrow. He'll pay you a visit."

"Ok, thank you, Josh," I said, not wanting him to go, but knowing he needed to.

The sheriff came back. He seemed to be friendlier when Josh wasn't around.

He offered me coffee. I didn't much like coffee, but I took it anyway. As we were drinking our coffee, he gave me his opinion on things. I kept in mind as he was talking that these were just his opinions, no one else's.

"Missy, let this old sheriff give you some advice, and also tell you some things you may not know. Joshua is a pretty good boy, but if I were a young girl like you, I'd think twice about a boy who counts on his daddy for everything. His daddy is governor of the state, you know. He used to be sheriff, was a sheriff for many years until he took the notion to run for governor. I'll be damned—excuse me, I mean darned—if he didn't up and win the race. He acts all high and mighty now and forgets about the days we used to go hunting in the woods. Why, him and me would see who could piss the farthest!"

He cleared his throat in embarrassment. "Oh, excuse me, I guess I'm not using proper talk for a lady. Anyway, what I'm getting at is the lad is spoiled rotten and he is a mama's boy to boot." The sheriff folded his arms and rested them on his big belly.

"Thank you, sheriff for letting me know these things, I'll keep them in mind," I told the sheriff.

But I knew full well I wasn't going to let this sheriff influence me about Josh. I was playing the life game of chess. The sheriff could be one of my important chess pieces. Being agreeable with the sheriff was just playing the game. I would play the game smart, like Grandpa had taught me. I would never lie, and I would never cheat. I would also think about every move.

I surprised myself by having a restful night sleep. When I woke up, I felt very hopeful about my future. I washed up the best I could. I then sat and prayed for all my loved ones. I also prayed that this ordeal would be over soon. Josh did not show up that morning or that afternoon. My heart felt heavy. I was beginning to worry. Just when I was about to ask Dullie if he had seen Josh, he walked in.

It was six thirty in the evening. Josh looked dirty and worn out.

Josh came over to my cell and said, "I'm sorry, Evie, I just couldn't make it here this morning. Dullie had me out doing all kinds of things. It seemed like he was trying his best to keep me away from here. I figured he couldn't keep me from seeing you on my own time, so here I am."

"Oh, thank you for coming, Joshua. I was getting really worried about you."

"I was afraid you'd be worried. I wish I could have gotten word to you that I would be later visiting you today. Evie, I can't wait until the day comes when I'm sheriff. Then I can be my own boss. But for now I have to mind Dullie. A deputy could get fired for not following orders. I sure got aggravated at Dullie though," Josh said, shaking his head.

"I wouldn't want you to get fired because of me," I told Josh.

"Don't worry about that," he answered back.

"Here, I brought us some dinner," Josh said as he lifted up a basket.

"Oh Josh, you shouldn't have," I said, but feeling really glad he did. I was very hungry.

"Well, it's nothing fancy. I just fixed us some ham and biscuits left over from breakfast. I also packed some of grandma's apple oatmeal cookies."

The food Josh took from the basket looked like a feast to me.

I joked with Josh and said, "You are going to make me fat bringing me all this wonderful food, what with me in jail getting no exercise."

"Evie, you have a long way to go before you get fat," Josh answered with a chuckle. "Besides, you need to keep your strength up. We have some real important days coming around the corner. My brother Steven will be here tomorrow. He will be happy to represent you a week from Tuesday. That is when your court date is, by the way. We just got word today."

My heart sank. When I realized I would be in jail another whole week, I couldn't hold back letting Josh know how I felt. "Oh my, Josh. I had no idea I would be in jail this long."

"I know, Evie. I tried to get the court date moved up. The court system is what it is. If a court date is scheduled, it's almost written in stone and very hard to change. I sure am sorry."

We ate our biscuits and ham in silence, both wondering what lie ahead. Dullie interrupted our silence. He had a plate of food in his hand; it looked to be greasy bacon and burnt fried potatoes.

"Hey! Feeding the prisoner is my job," Dullie said gruffly.

Evie

"Well, from the looks of what's on that plate you are not doing a very good job," Josh observed. "I wouldn't feed that to my worst enemy."

Dullie mumbled under his breath—something about how he wondered how Josh's daddy would feel after finding out his son took up with an outlaw. He walked away, continuing to mumble. We heard him open the back door of the jail, toss the food outside, and whistle for the town's strays.

Josh hugged me and said, "Sorry."

He gathered up the basket, squeezed my hand, and whispered that this would all be over soon. He walked up to the front of the jail house/ I heard more arguing between Dullie and Josh. I heard a door slam. I knew Josh had left angry. I said a silent prayer, praying Josh would not get fired because of me.

It wasn't easy sitting in this cell. The only thing I had to read was the Bible. I like reading the Bible, but not all day long. I was left alone for many hours with my thoughts and, of course, my prayers. I realize I need to adjust my attitude. I needed to think about the lessons Grandpa had taught me about my life. Sometimes a person just needs to sit patient and wait for the right timing on things. If the court said I need to wait a week, well, then there must be a reason. Mama always said a righteous man's steps are ordered by God.

I will trust and pray everything works out for the best.

Chapter 23

On Saturday, I met with Josh's brother, Steven. Steven looked a lot like Josh, only older. He seemed very wise. He got right down to business. He read the notes Josh took and asked me many questions.

After the questions, he said, "Miss Thompson, I see no reason your innocence cannot be proven. I am going to be doing some investigating. I will be back mid-week."

"Thank you, Mr. Harrison. I don't know how to thank you. This means so much."

"Miss Thompson, my job is to prove innocence. I expose injustice. and that's just what we have here." Steven Harrison bowed slightly and said, "Until we meet again, Miss Thompson." He turned on his heels and left.

The next day was Sunday. I woke up and asked for some fresh water for bathing. It had become a ritual for the sheriff to hang the blanket for privacy. I came to realize the sheriff was a contradiction; he was a grouchy angry man around Josh, but he was kind to me. There was actually something very enduring about him. He seemed to really care about my privacy. For that, I was grateful.

Later that Sunday, I heard a shocking sound. I heard Al Jenkins' voice! From what I could overhear, he wanted to see me, but the sheriff refused. He said it was against the law for the one pressing charges to converse with the prisoner. He had been in to see me once before.

He must have snuck in, I thought. I remember no one else was in the jail house. I was grateful there were bars between him and me. I then heard Al Jenkins tell the sheriff he had seen me when I had first arrived. The sheriff loudly accused him of breaking the law by sneaking into the jailhouse and speaking to a prisoner. He threatened to arrest him if he didn't leave.

"She is my daughter!" Al Jenkins shouted.

"Well, the way I recall it, she is J.C. and Laura Thompson's daughter, not yours," the sheriff argued.

"We will just see what the court says about that," Al sneered. Then he left.

I felt great relief when Al Jenkins left. His very presence makes my skin crawl. Even before I knew he was in the jailhouse, I felt an evil uneasy feeling. It was almost as if he was the devil himself. I shuddered again and willed myself not to think of the Evil Al Jenkins.

Nothing much happened for the next few days. I knew it had been raining outside, so I didn't feel quite as bad locked up in the cell, but most days I really missed outside. I craved sunshine.

Josh showed up on Tuesday night. He looked very concerned when he saw at me.

"What's wrong, Evie? You're looking pale."

"Oh, Josh, I know I've only been held up in this cell for a little while, but I really miss the sunshine. I miss the warmth on my skin. I miss hearing the birds sing. I miss the evening breeze blowing my hair."

My eyes filled with tears.

Josh looked stern for a moment and then said, "Evie. the way I see it, the prisoner needs exercise. Come on, I'm taking you out for an evening stroll."

He grabbed my hand and led me right out of the cell.

"Oh, Josh do you mean it? Will we get in trouble? I can't believe I'm finally going outside."

I was so excited that I realized I had been rambling.

Josh smiled. "You won't be able to see sunshine, but you can feel the evening breeze in your hair."

"Oh, Josh, I can't wait!"

"There is one more thing, Evie. I need to keep you handcuffed to me at all times."

Evie

Josh and I looked at each other. He had a twinkle in his eye.

"Ok, Josh, I understand," I answered with a smile.

I felt so excited about going outside that I could hardly contain myself. Before we walked out of the jailhouse, Josh, true to his word, handcuffed us together.

"I'd really get in trouble if I didn't do this. Besides," Josh winked, "it gives me an excuse to be close to you."

We walked out the front door of the jailhouse. Luckily, the sheriff had gone home for a few hours, so we didn't have to argue about what we were doing. It was dark out. The evening breeze was like heaven. I stood and breathed in the freshness of the air. I once took breathing fresh air for granted; I never will again as long as I live.

Josh and I walked around the jailhouse many times. He said he didn't want to stray too far. He didn't want people to take notice. Someone would tell the sheriff and he would have to go around and around with Dullie, and he just wasn't up to it. On our last trip around the jailhouse, we stopped near a large oak tree near the back of the building. Josh stopped leaned against the oak tree and pulled me close to him.

"Evie, I'm so sorry you are locked up in that cell. Steven is working hard to get you out of there."

Josh pulled me close. We stayed leaned up against that tree for the longest time. Finally, Josh spoke up and said, "Evie, I know we are taking a chance coming out here like this, but I just couldn't stand to see you cry."

"Thank you, Josh," I said. I laid my head on his chest.

Josh's free arm came around me. I heard the beating of his heart. His arms felt strong around me, and I felt so safe. Gently, he leaned in and kissed me on the lips, a very soft kiss. Then he kissed me on the forehead.

He then held me closer, rested his head on mine, and whispered, "I can't wait to get you away from this place."

Suddenly, we heard the sheriff's loud voice, "What on God's green earth do you think you are doing out here?"

Dullie shouted so loud I think the whole town could have heard him.

Josh pulled us away from the tree, unintentionally still holding my hand that was handcuffed to his. His face was bright red. I couldn't tell if he was embarrassed, mad, or both.

"Dullie, come on! Evie needed some fresh air!" Josh protested. "She hadn't had fresh air in over a week. She also needed some exercise to get her legs moving around."

"You look like you were giving her more than fresh air, and she looked like she was liked everything you was giving her," Dullie said with a smirk on his face. "I sure hope you don't have you one of those girls like they have hanging out at Ernie's place."

Suddenly, Josh reached into his pocket, grabbed the handcuff keys, and unlocked himself from me. He marched over and grabbed the sheriff by the shirt.

"No, Joshua!" I shouted.

"Stand back, Evie. I will not have him insulting you like that."

Before I could say any more, Josh hit the sheriff square in the jaw.

The sheriff fell backward. Blood squirted everywhere.

I screamed, "Oh my Lord!"

"Ok, sonny boy. You have done it now! You are out a job! Just try crawling back to your daddy. He'll have a hard time defending you on this one."

"Well, since I don't have a job, what do I have to lose?" Josh shouted. Then he hit the sheriff again.

"Your freedom, that's what!" the sheriff shouted. He took the handcuff off me and put Josh's hands behind his back and cuffed him. "You are under arrest for assaulting an officer."

"Please, sheriff, don't arrest him!" I pleaded. "He was just looking out for me."

"His looking out for you just got him in a heap of trouble," the sheriff shouted back.

Josh looked at me and said, "I'm sorry Evie."

It seemed as though he wanted to say more, but the sheriff jerked him away and motioned for me to follow. He walked us back into the jailhouse. Josh was locked into the cell next to mine.

"Now see if you can behave yourselves. I need to make a phone call. It will be interesting hearing how that big shot daddy of yours will take to this news," the sheriff said with a smirk.

He walked away laughing.

"Joshua?" I asked hesitantly after a few minutes of silence.

"Evie, I'm sorry. I know I shouldn't have hit him, but I couldn't stand him degrading you like that. You just didn't deserve it. You don't deserve any of this."

"But now you are in trouble," I said to him. "Don't worry. After I explain to my father and Steven, I'll be out of here in no time at all. I think sometimes Dullie lives to give me a hard time."

"But now you don't have a job."

"Don't worry. I'll get it back" Josh said.

Evie

We sat in silence for a long while. Me in my cell and Josh in his. We heard the sheriff on the phone. He was speaking loudly. We couldn't make out exactly what he was saying. It seemed he was trying to reach Josh's father. We then heard the door slam. We knew we were alone.

"Josh, why does the sheriff have it out for you?" I asked.

"He doesn't. He has it out for my father," Josh answered.

"Why?" I asked.

Joshua was silent for a moment. Then he began telling me the story.

"It wasn't always that way. They used to be friends. They grew up together."

As Joshua was talking, I walked over to the cell bars to try and see him. He was sitting on the cell floor with his back and head leaned up against the bars. I too sat on the floor and leaned against the bars. We sat and talked this way for what seemed like hours.

"Daddy was always one up on Dullie," he said. "He was better at fishing, hunting, baseball, everything. Daddy never wanted things to be a competition between him and Dullie, but Dullie made everything a competition. He would say, 'Hey I bet I can catch more fish than you or I bet I kill a

205

deer and you don't.' All this competition seemed like kid stuff but then when they were in high school, and both fell for the same girl. Daddy won and ended up with Barbara Miller, who happens to be my mom. Years later, they both ran for sheriff, and of course daddy won by a land slide. Some people thought Dullie only ran because he wanted to beat Daddy at something, only it made matters worse because Daddy won the nomination by a landslide. Dullie has held a grudge ever since. So, something like this, me getting arrested and all, makes Dullie feel really good."

"Oh, how sad," I said.

"I don't know about sad. It's ridiculous if you ask me. It will end up backfiring on Dullie like it always does. I'll tell Steven how he mistreated the prisoner by accusing her of ill repute. The state will file charges, which will cause Dullie to drop his charges. It might not even amount to that. The threat might be all it takes."

"Why do you call him Dullie? Is that his actual name?" I asked.

"It's his nickname," Josh explained.

"What is his real name?" I asked.

"It's Ralph Dullian. When he was a kid, all the guys called him Dullie. I'm sure he would rather I call him Mr. Dullian. But I call him Dullie like everyone else."

Evie

"Speaking of Dullie, I think he is back in the jailhouse," I warned.

Dullie came back to our cell and spoke to Josh, "Your Papa wasn't pleased to hear what you done, boy. I don't think you are going to get out of this one so easy. You'll think twice before striking an officer of the law again."

"Maybe the officer should think twice before he insults a lady," Josh answered back angrily.

"What lady?" the sheriff asked. Then he looked at me. He must have seen the hurt in my eyes. It did offend me that he would suggest I wasn't a lady.

He then came over to my cell and whispered, "I'm sorry, Miss Evie, I reckon you're about as much of a lady as I've ever known. I'm just trying to rile the boy."

I shook my head in understanding, feeling all this behavior was very silly and unnecessary but also a little humorous.

Dullie announced, "Lights out."

The cell went pitch black.

"You could have given us fair warning, Dullie," Josh shouted.

"Evie, are you ok?"

"Yes. I'll just feel my way around."

207

As I lay in my cell, I felt greatly uncomfortable. My bladder was full. I wish I would have had a chance to relieve myself. I felt too embarrassed to ask because Josh was in the next cell.

It was almost as if Josh could read my thoughts because he said, "Dullie did it ever cross your mind that the prisoners might have human needs to take care of?"

Dullie turned back on the light and walked back to my cell. "My apologies, Miss Evie. Would you like me to escort you outside?"

"Yes, I would, sir," I answered, feeling embarrassed, yet relieved.

After a short time, I was back in. The jailhouse lights were again turned off.

"Goodnight, Joshua," I said.

"Goodnight, Evie," he answered quietly.

The next morning, Josh's brother Steven came and did a thing called "bailing out." Josh explained it to me; he said it's when someone comes to the jailhouse and pays money to get someone they know out of jail. I told Josh I didn't think I knew anyone rich enough to bail me out. He said he didn't think a person could get bailed out if they were in prison for murder. Somehow, knowing this made me feel even more desperate and anxious to get out of here.

Evie

After Steven bailed Josh out, the lawyer came into my cell to speak with me.

"I found out some pertinent information concerning your case," he said.

I didn't want to sound foolish, but I really needed to know what the word "pertinent" meant, so I asked him. If he thought I was foolish, he didn't act like it.

"It means 'relevant,' or 'important,' if you will. It is information that could help on your defense at your trial." He went on to explain that old man Cains spotted me running faster than a lightning bolt up the road. "To put it in old man Cains' words," Steven added.

Old Man Cains is a wiry ninety-year-old man who lives near the Smiths' house. He used to be the town blacksmith, but since everyone started using cars instead of horse and buggy, it put him out of business in town. He now has a little shop in the barn.

Steven went on to explain that Cains was curious to see where I was going in such a hurry. He jumped on his horse and made his way to the Smiths' house.

"He figured you must have been really anxious for a visit. The important information I gathered from Cains, however, is the timeframe in which you were spotted at the Smiths' house. He said he saw you enter their house at 9:00 am and leave at 9:30 am. The town doctor and undertaker said the Smiths were dead long before 9:00. The interesting thing is this Cains fellow saw your father's truck drive down the road about midnight. Cains was checking on one of his mares. He shined a light on the pickup. Al Jenkins was in your father's pickup driving away from the Smith's house."

"Oh my," I gasped.

In my mind, I was picturing a chess board. The pieces had people's faces on them. Steven's piece moved. He was closing in on Evil Al. Steven was the white knight and Evil Al was the evil black king.

"Miss Thompson, are you listening to me?"

"Yes," I answered, coming out of my daydreaming.

Steven continued to explain, "If we could convince Cains to repeat to the court what he said to me, it would be most excellent."

"Yes, it would," I said.

"Miss Thompson, I need to get back to Chicago. However, Joshua will be working as a detective on your case. I will be back for the trial. Steven turned to leave but I could not let him leave without asking about Josh."

"Mr. Harrison!" I called out.

Steven turned around and answered, "Yes Miss Thompson?"

"Did Josh get his deputy job back?" Steven smiled slightly and answered, "No. We did, however, get the sheriff to drop the charges."

I wanted to ask more questions but, before I could form them, Steven said, "As I said earlier, he is doing detective work. Until later." Steven bowed slightly. Then he went on his way.

When he left, my mind started to imagine again. I imagined Joshua as the white king and, of course, I was the queen. I smiled to myself.

Chapter 24

There were only two more days until the trial. I was feeling nervous, hoping and praying the court would see the truth. It was Sunday afternoon. I was laying on the cot, reading from the book of Matthew, when the sheriff came in and announced I had visitors. I stood up wondering who it could be.

Then Grandpa came walking in, and behind him were John and Beth.

"Oh my," I said. I couldn't stop the tears from flowing. I was so happy to see Grandpa and my dear friends, Brother John and Beth. The Sheriff let them come into my cell, and we all hugged.

"Listen, Evie," John said, "we are here on a social call, but there is some business I need to discuss with you as well."

"You'll be mighty happy to hear what they found out, gal," Grandpa added.

John held up his hand as if to say, *Wait a minute. Let's tell her slowly.*

Evie

Brother John began explaining, "Evie, we men of God are all kind of interconnected. I've come to know many pastors, ministers, brothers, and priests through the years. If you are truly a man of God, it doesn't take too long to spot a phony. I started asking some of the good men I met in the past about Al Jenkins. It turns out Al Jenkins has a past, and there are a lot of folks after him. He has been hard to hunt down because he keeps changing his name. Seems he has had three wives that we know of, not including your mother. There may even be more."

I sat with my mouth wide open. I couldn't believe my ears. I was relieved yet sad at the same time. I felt relief that my innocence would now be more easily proven but sad that my own mother fell victim to his evil schemes. Brother John waited a while before he continued. I think he was giving me time to let his news sink in. I nodded my head, letting him know I would like him to continue

Brother John read what I meant and continued.

"When he enters a new town, he pretends to be a minister of God's word. He does good deeds, visits and prays for the sick, and speaks kindly to everyone until they trust and come to care for him. He strategically finds a widow or an old maid and begins his conquest. He gets everything he can from the poor, unsuspecting women, even her life. There was one town where he did not come in as a minister, but as a teacher. However, most of the time he disguised himself as a preacher. It must have come easier for him. Yes, Al Jenkins is a fraud."

We all sat in silence for a moment, wondering how a human being could be so evil.

Brother John spoke up again. "He was almost arrested in the town he was in before he came to here. He fled the town and changed his name. No one knows for sure what his real name is.

"How did you figure out it was him?" I asked.

Brother John answered me quickly, "Good question. Some of us started putting two and two together. Also, we needed a lot of prayer. I feel we had help from the Lord. I'm sure the good Lord is tired of His children being hurt and killed by this evil man."

Grandpa looked madder than a green-eyed wasp. "My daughter and grand-daughter have been some of those people. He has to be stopped! He is like the devil himself."

"But listen," John continued, "this guy is not only evil. He is also intelligent. This is a dangerous combination. That's why this guy is still around; he outsmarts everyone. Well, we are going to outsmart him. It seems he is in no hurry to leave this area. As you know, Evie, he has settled into your family's home. He has no right to it, but he thinks he has every right to it. He can't have any suspicions that we are on to his tactics, or he will be out of here fast. Evie, I hear you have a very reliable lawyer on your side."

"Yes, I do," I answered numbly, still trying to take in all this information I had been given. Suddenly, I felt an urgent need for Josh's brother to hear all of this information.

"Oh, Brother John, my lawyer Steven Harrison has to hear all of this, and soon!"

"Those are my thoughts exactly. How could I get a hold of him?" Brother John asked.

I had a card with Mr. Harrison's name and number. I gave it to Brother John. He said he would call him right away. The sheriff came back to my cell and announced that our visitation time was up. We all hugged each other. Then they were on their way.

It was sad to see them leave, but I felt an overwhelming sense of relief that everything was going to be ok. I had a good feeling Evil Al would no longer be able to hurt anyone else. I felt all the pieces in my chess game of life were lining up in just the right order.

Chapter 25

The day of the trial was finally here! My lawyer, Mr. Harrison, visited earlier in the day. He said his talk with Brother John was very interesting, to say the least. He also informed me that Josh's investigation of Al Jenkins was very interesting. It actually confirmed what Brother John found out about Al Jenkins. Al Jenkins wasn't really this evil man's name; his real name was, possibly, Robert Sucadas. He had used at least fifteen aliases since naming himself Al Jenkins.

Mr. Harrison continued, "Evie, this trial is to prove your innocence, not to prove Al Jenkins guilty of murder. That will come later, I assure you."

I nodded in understanding. Deep down, I would not feel totally peaceful until Evil Al Jenkins, whatever his real name, was behind bars—for Mama's sake, and for every other person he had hurt or whose life he had destroyed.

The sheriff drove me to the courthouse, which was a few blocks away. I could have just set out walking, but I guess it was "procedure," as the sheriff put it, to officially deliver the prisoner to the courthouse. I tried to look the best I could. I washed and brushed my hair, and the sheriff had somehow found me a better fitting dress. It was much better fit than the tent of a dress I had been given when I arrived, but I still needed to tighten it with a belt.

As I walked into the courthouse, I was surprised to see practically the whole town was there. Everyone turned and looked at me. I heard a bunch of murmuring; it seemed they were all talking at once. I walked down to the front of the courthouse. Josh and his brother were there to greet me. They both stood up; Josh gave me a quick hug, Steven nodded. We sat down. The court room was still loud with murmuring. Finally, I heard the judge say, "Order in the court."

Crack! The judge slammed the gavel down on the desk.

I looked around the court room. Then I saw him: Evil Al. He was glaring at me with those dark, beady eyes. I quickly looked away. I could not stand to look at him: he was the reason I was in prison and going through this hardship. He is the reason I didn't have a mama. Mama always said, "Pray for your enemies."

All I prayed for Evil Al is that he would get what is coming to him.

Finally, the court room quieted. I glanced at the jury; there were ten members, five women and five men, all different ages. They were looking at me. I looked down, unsure of whether I was to look at them or not. The bailiff announced what the trial was about:

"The State of Illinois versus Evelyn Thompson, arrested for murder on the eleventh of September for the murders of Opal and Leonard Smith."

It was shocking to me to hear what I was accused of doing. It seemed so official and everything. I began shaking; I was nervous and sad at the same time. I felt nervous because all this was so intimidating! I hope I have a fair jury. I felt sad because I cared so much for the Smiths and just hearing again about the murder and the fact that I was accused brought tears to my eyes. I willed myself not to cry but I could not help it; tears began to flow.

Mr. Harrison handed me a hankie and told me to contain myself. I wiped my eyes, turned around, and noticed Grandpa, Brother John, and Beth. They all looked at me with concern, and maybe even a little pity. I tried to smile; they smiled back, as if to say everything would be okay. Earlier, Steven had told me that Grandpa, Brother John, and Old Man Cain's were going to be called as witnesses. He also said that a witness was to testify against me. It wasn't a mystery who that person might be. I knew exactly who it was, and he was still staring at me. I looked down to avoid his stare.

Evie

Suddenly, I heard a voice say, "Alexander Jenkins come to the stand, please."

He walked up took his place and once again glared at me and smiled.

In my mind, I was picturing my chess game of life. All the pieces were moving into the appropriate place. I would win this game, but I hadn't won yet. This was the end of this particular game and it had to be played with clever moves and clever timing. My "day-dreaming" about chess stopped when Evil Al spoke; everything he said was a lie.

He told the court that I had been a troubled child ever since his poor wife passed away. It made me sick to my stomach to watch him; he was so fake! He tried to convince the jury he was a heartbroken husband who had tried his best to make me behave and become a productive citizen in the community. He said it was no use, that I was more than he could handle. The only truthful thing he said was that I couldn't get along with him. When the court asked him if I ever brought up Opal and Leonard Smith, the lie he answer with made me angry. I don't think I had ever felt such anger in all my life.

"Yes, this is very troubling for me," he answered the question in his fake emotional voice. "One night, when she was having one of her anger fits, she told me she wanted to live somewhere away from here. Away from me."

Oh, brother, I thought as I watched his theatrics! He even wiped away fake tears.

He continued, "She said she wanted to live at the Smith's home, but the only way she could live there was if they were dead."

How could he flat-out lie like that? I began to shake. I could not hold back. I stood up and shouted, "That's a boldface lie! I never said that!"

Steven quickly stood up, grabbed my shoulders, and sat me back in my seat.

"There will be no more outbursts in the court!" the judge said loudly. He hit his gavel on his desk and said, "We will have a ten-minute recess. We will resume at three-sharp."

Steven sat beside me and said, "Evelyn, I know this is very hard, but you must control yourself."

"I'm sorry. I just couldn't stand hearing those lies, and he is so good at it," I said, feeling regretful.

"Don't worry, the truth will be proven," Steven assured me.

Josh was sitting beside Steven mouthing, "It will be ok."

Looking at Josh's handsome face and hearing those words gave me the calm I needed.

The trial resumed with the district attorney calling a few more of Evil Al's yes men to the bench. Knowing they were under oath made these simple-minded men nervous. It turns out they could not state anything as fact, only hearsay, on behalf of the man they were so devoted to, Al Jenkins. Mr. Harrison made this point very clear when he cross-examined the men. The men would get nervous and admit they knew little about the case, only what Al Jenkins told them.

"No more questions," Steven said.

It was our turn to go to the stand now. I mentally moved my chess pieces. Steven called Grandpa to the stand. Grandpa spoke with grace and dignity and told of how I had relayed the story to him. He described how devastated I was to find Opal and Lenard dead.

"Objections, your honor. This too is hearsay," the district attorney said.

"Objection overruled," the judge said.

"Thank you, your honor," Steven said.

"Please continue," Steven said to my grandpa.

Grandpa continued talking and shared how I was so helpful around the house.

"Objection, your honor. The material is not relevant to the case," the district attorney argued. The judge agreed and Grandpa was dismissed from the bench.

Brother John was called to the stand. Mr. Harrison began asking him questions on how he met me. He told them how he found me alone on the steps of his church, how he invited me to he and his wife's home. He told the court how I opened up about what I had been through. The district attorney looked like he wanted to object again. However, he waited to cross-examine Brother John himself.

"Isn't it true, Brother Sanders, that Evelyn Thompson seemed to be running from something? Trying to get away?"

Brother John was very wise his response. "Evelyn Thompson was not trying to run away *from* something as much as she was trying to get *to* something. She was desperately trying to get to the safety of her grandfather's home."

"Why was she trying to get to her grandfather's home?" the district attorney asked, obviously trying to trip Brother John.

Brother John answered quickly. "She was fleeing the abuse of her mother's new husband. This was her mother's desire."

Evie

Suddenly, there was a buzz in the court room. Everyone was looking at Evil Al. The chess pieces of my game of chess had just made a great move.

"Objection, your honor. The defendant just tried to deface someone in the court room."

"Sustained," the judge said.

After a few other questions, Brother John was released from the bench. Mr. Cains was then called up. As Mr. Cain walked to the bench, I was visualizing my chess game of life. I had many pawns on my side: Josh, Beth, the sheriff, and some town's people. They were all important, of course, but the more important pieces were the people that could actually make a difference in the trial. I saw myself as the queen, Steven as the power king piece, and Grandpa as the bishop. A bishop may move any number of vacant squares diagonally. The bishop is a predictable chess piece. You always knew what to expect from a bishop, as you could with Grandpa. Brother John was a knight; a knight moves in a very complicated way. I saw the knight as very intelligent. The knight sometimes saves the game.

Mr. Cains is my rook. A rook is the highest-ranking chess piece next to the king and queen. I felt Mr. Cains was going to prove to be very powerful in my case.

My hunch was right: Mr. Cains had actual facts about when he saw me enter and leave the Smith's house.

"Mr. Cains, I would like for you to explain to the jury exactly what you saw on the morning of April 19, 1949, the day the Smith's bodies were discovered." Mr. Harrison said in a direct voice.

"Well, it was a little before nine in the morning. I was tending to my horse, Maggie, when suddenly I saw Evelyn Thompson flying down the road faster than lightning. She was going as fast as her little legs could take her. I got on my horse to ride over to see why she was in such a hurry. It was exactly nine o'clock in the morning when she went through the Smith's door."

Mr. Harris interrupted by questioning. "How exactly did you know it was nine o'clock?"

"Well, I know this because I looked at my pocket watch."

"Thank you, Mr. Cains. Please continue."

"I decided to go on down the road to give Maggie a little exercise. When I came back up the road, I notice Evelyn leaving the Smith's house. I looked at my watch again. I was curious how long I had been riding Maggie. It was nine-twenty-five."

Evie

Thinking of my chess game again, I said "Check!" under my breath.

Mr. Harris turned towards the witness and said, "Thank you Mr. Cains." He then looked towards the Judge and said, "Your Honor, that is all I have for this witness."

The Judge looked at Mr. Cains and said, "Thank you Mr. Cains, you may step down."

The jury took about an hour to come up with a verdict. Everyone in my chess game of life was on edge. Josh kept giving me assuring smiles. I didn't turn around to look at Grandpa. I just didn't want to take the chance of crying. I sat silently and prayed; I had to get free. I needed justice for Mama.

As we were waiting for the jury to return to the court room, Mr. Harrison walked up to the judge and put several pieces of paper in front of him. The judge put on his glasses and read the papers; then he looked at me. I could have sworn I saw a smile on his face, but I wasn't quite sure.

The jury returned and a note was handed to the judge. The judge read the note. It was then handed back to the jury.

A juror stood and read the note, "We, the jury, find the defendant not guilty of the murders of Opal and Lenard Smith."

I put my head in my hands and cried with relief.

The judge continued, "In addition to Evelyn Thompson's innocent verdict, she is also released from being under the guardianship of Alexander Jenkins. Furthermore, she is the legal owner of her parent's property and its contents. She may return to the residence with a proper guardian."

"I object!" a loud voice said.

"Mr. Jenkins, you are not in a position to object. You must remain silent," the judge stated.

Al Jenkins ignored the judge's command. "I was legally married to Laura Thompson! I have the rightful ownership of her the property and her daughter!"

The judge hit his gavel on the bench and said sternly, "I will have order in this court, or you will be escorted out of here. Is that clear, Mr. Jenkins?"

Al Jenkins did not answer the judge, but he did sit down.

The judge then called Mr. Harrison to the bench to address the court. "The court has in its possession a legal birth certificate stating that Evelyn Thompson is the legal daughter to a man in the courtroom."

The courtroom became a buzz of conversation again. The judge hit his gavel hard on the bench. The courtroom fell

Evie

silent. I noticed that Al Jenkins had a look of triumph on his face.

Oh, how I love my life game of chess! I thought. *You are soon going to have the surprise move of your life, Evil Al.*

Mr. Harrison continued. "The man in the courtroom who is the legal father of Evelyn Thompson is not Alexander Jenkins. Evelyn's biological and legal father is William Owens."

Once again, the courtroom was abuzz, and once again the judge hit the gavel down. The judge ordered Steven to proceed.

"The court also has in its possession a deed and a will that states, in the occurrence of the death of her parents, Evelyn Thompson shall be awarded all properties. These documents have been signed by Laura Thompson, Evelyn's mother."

"No!" Al Jenkins shouted. He ran up to the front of the courtroom and tried to grab the documents, but Josh was quick and grabbed his arm. Al Jenkins pulled his arm away from Josh and lunged towards me. The judge stood and slammed his gavel down.

"Order in the court!" he demanded. "Deputy, arrest this man!" The judge ordered, pointing at Al Jenkins. "Mr. Jenkins, you are being arrested for disorderly conduct."

It took five men to handcuff Al Jenkins; it was as if he turned into a wild animal. He kept yelling, "It's all lies, I tell you! You are all damn liars!"

He was taken away from the courthouse shouting obscenities, wanting us all to rot in hell. I couldn't help thinking what a sad contrast he was to the man he pretended to be. He pretended to win souls to Christ, now he was damning them to hell.

Mr. Harrison addressed the judge: "May I have a moment with you, your honor?"

"We have no need for private conversation; address the court with what you have to say," the judge ordered.

Steven addressed the court as he was ordered, "I have information that was to be brought to legal attention after the trial of Evelyn Thompson; however, considering the events which have occurred at this trial, the information in my hands would be appropriately revealed at this time. There has been enough evidence to arrest Al Jenkins for the murders of Opal and Lenard Smith."

The courtroom was again loud with conversation. The judge hit his gavel but didn't bother quieting the courtroom.

Instead, he shouted, "Al Jenkins is under arrest not only for disorderly conduct but for the deaths of Opal and Lenard Smith."

Evie

He looked at me. "Evelyn Thompson, you are a free woman. This courtroom is dismissed."

The judge stepped down, wiping the sweat from his brow.

"Check," I said out loud, not really caring who heard me.

The day will come when I will be able to say, "Checkmate"—when Evil Al is convicted and behind bars for life.

Chapter 26

Before I left the courthouse, Mr. Harrison handed me a set of keys. The keys were to Daddy's truck and the farmhouse. He got them from Al Jenkins before he was carted off to the State prison. He explained that Al Jenkins had gotten Daddy's truck out of the ditch where I had left it. He got it running again and had been driving it ever since. In my hands were the keys to what Mama and Daddy had worked so hard for.

As I left the courthouse, Josh's Mama and Daddy were waiting outside the door. They both hugged me. They had come to town for the trial. Having heard all the details of my case, they became very interested and were very happy with the outcome of the trial. Josh's Daddy said it was a time for celebration; he invited everyone out to dinner. Grandpa, being a proud man, declined, but he reconsidered when I pleaded with him to come.

Thankfully, Grandpa was a man of faith and had believed I would be set free. He brought my extra clothes from home so I would have something to change into. I promptly went back to the jailhouse and took off the oversized scratchy prison dress. I slid my clean cotton dress on. It felt so wonderful.

Josh introduced himself to Grandpa during dinner. I felt sorry for Josh; he seemed so nervous; he kept stammering over his words. Grandpa looked over at me and winked.

He then leaned over and whispered, "This boy is lovestruck bad, ain't he?"

I felt myself blush and looked away. Grandpa smiled and chuckled to himself.

We all had a wonderful dinner, even Brother John and Beth joined us. Sadly, after dinner, they bid me farewell with hugs and promises of seeing me again. They had become such dear friends. God had directed me to their doorstep. I shudder to think what would have happened to me if I had not met them. I said a silent prayer, asking God to let me see them again someday.

With my arm linked into Grandpa's arm, we walked to his truck. I began bracing myself for the emotional experience of walking into the home I grew up in. Grandpa, sensing my feelings, grabbed my hand and said, "Now, Evie, I plan on staying as long as you need me to. I know you need someone to stand by your side for a spell. I figure the best person to do that would be kinfolk, and that's what I am. I asked Jacob

231

Sperry down the road to watch my place; he said he was happy to do it."

"Thank you so much, Grandpa," I cried and hugged him with thankfulness.

"Well now, you are my young'un. I've got some lost time to make up for anyhow," Grandpa added with a sad, faraway look in his eyes.

To my delight, when I climbed into Grandpa's truck, I noticed he had brought Poker, his dog.

"Oh Poker!" I shouted. Poker greeted me with licks all over my face.

Grandpa and I were just getting ready to head down the road when Josh ran up to Grandpa's truck, as if he were afraid he would miss his chance.

"Excuse me Mr. Owens; I was wondering if I could have your permission to come visit Evie tomorrow?"

Grandpa looked over at me with a twinkle in his eye and said, "I don't know Evie, what do you think?"

"It would be fine with me," I answered.

Grandpa sat quite for a minute. Then he said, "I tell you what: how about you give Evie a day or so to settle in, then come for a visit. I figure the day after tomorrow should be a good."

"Yes, sir." Josh nodded. "The day after tomorrow then."

With a big smile, Josh waved us on our way.

As Grandpa, Poker, and I were traveling down the familiar road, I felt excitement. I was finally going home. Grandpa had the windows down. I breathed the fresh, familiar scent of the country. For the first time in a long time, I felt safe and free from danger. Realizing I would be home soon and sleeping in my own bed made me tired. I found myself drifting. I heard Grandpa's voice asking me for directions. Suddenly, it dawned on me that he did not know where the family farm was. I sleepily gave him directions.

As we drove up to the house, I didn't have the welcoming feeling I thought I would have. Instead, I had a feeling of trepidation that something was wrong. Every light in the house was on; it was lit up like a Christmas tree. As we pulled up further into the yard, the lights were turned off one by one. Grandpa must have felt a bad feeling too, because he no sooner pulled into the driveway than he started backing up again.

"What's wrong, Grandpa?" I shouted.

"Before them lights went out, I saw a man with a gun standing at the window," Grandpa said as he urgently pulled into the street. "We ain't walking into that trap"

The man with the gun suddenly ran out the front door and started shooting.

"Hurry Grandpa!" I shouted as the bullets struck the truck.

A bullet struck our back window, which shattered all over us! I quickly brushed the glass off and checked Grandpa and me; we looked to only have a few cuts. Poker was going crazy; he was barking and growling and jumping up and down. Grandpa pushed hard on the gas and we shot off down the street.

A few more shots rang out from the house, but then they stopped. We were safe.

"How in the world those bullets kept from missing our heads, I'll never know," Grandpa said between heavy breaths.

"I know how, Grandpa, because The Good Lord was looking out for us."

We quickly drove back into town to the sheriff's office. Grandpa, Poker, and me jumped out of the truck. We checked ourselves over to make sure we didn't have a bad cut somewhere. Grandpa took and old rag he had in the back of the truck and racked the glass out of the front seat.

Evie

We walked into the jailhouse; Dullie was there along with the new deputy.

The sheriff took one look at us and asked, "What in tarnation happened to ya'll?"

Grandpa and I looked at each other, we both had little cuts all over our arms and a few on our face and neck. The new deputy handed us each a wet cloth.

"Ya'll better put alcohol on them sores before they fester," Dullie said, looking at us and waiting for us to explain.

"Someone was at Momma and Daddy's house, and they shot at us," I explained.

Suddenly, Josh ran into the jailhouse looking very worried. He grabbed me and said, "Evie, thank God you are all right! I saw your grandpa's truck all shot up; it scared the living daylights out of me."

I melted into Josh's arms. It scared me something fierce that we got shot at. I wanted to feel Josh's strong arms around me.

Grandpa explained to Josh what had happened.

"I'm going out there!" Josh shouted.

"You'll do no such thing; you ain't the law!" Dullie shouted. "At least not here."

Dullie pointed at the new deputy with his big thumb. "Me and Tim here, we'll go out there and see what this is all about. Why don't you take your girl and her grandpappy to the hotel? They both had a long day and need a good night sleep. The dog can hang out here at the jailhouse."

Dullie leaned over to pet Poker.

Poker growled and showed his teeth.

Dullie pulled his hand back. "Friendly mutt, ain't he?" he said sarcastically.

Grandpa said he would just as soon hang out at the jailhouse. He said he wouldn't be able to sleep until he found out what was going on at his granddaughter's house. It seemed odd to hear Grandpa refer to Momma and Daddy's house as mine. I suppose it is mine and rightly so. Suddenly, I felt angry that someone was trespassing on my property. I knew I would not be able to sleep either. I asked if Grandpa, Poker, and I could just be at the jailhouse until we got to the bottom of why a gunman was at my house. Dullie agreed it would be the best place for us.

Josh convinced Dullie that he would need more men than just him and Tim to go where a gunman was held up. Dullie reluctantly agreed and they rounded up some more men in town. The sheriff temporarily deputized them all. They were all assigned guns; one after the other they filed out of the jailhouse. Josh was the last one out the door, after giving me a hug and reassuring me everything would be okay.

Evie

"Grandpa, I'm scared. I don't want harm to come to anyone."

"Evelyn, that man at your place is outnumbered. He'll come out with his hands up." Grandpa paused for a minute. "I was thinking maybe I should go along with those men and help defend my granddaughter's home."

It seemed Grandpa was asking me if it was ok if he went. I begged him not to go. I told him I didn't want to lose anyone else. Saying this convinced him to stay with Poker and me. I prayed hard there would be no bloodshed. I didn't want Josh to go, but I knew there would be no stopping him. Upholding justice was who Josh is; it was in his blood.

It was approaching eleven o' clock. I was so weary from the trying day that I couldn't keep my eyes open. I laid my head on Poker and fell fast asleep. I dreamt of Mamma and Daddy. They were holding hands; Mamma looked so happy. She was smiling her real smile. Daddy looked proud; he told me he was proud of me. He said I should stay strong because I was almost home. Mamma was saying something too.

"What, Mamma?" I asked.

She faintly said she was so sorry she wasn't with me, but she was glad I was with Grandpa. Mamma and Daddy began to fade.

"No! Don't go, Mamma. Daddy, please don't go!" I shouted, reaching out to them.

I opened my eyes to find Grandpa standing over me, saying "It's okay, Evie, you must have had a bad dream. I'm here young'un. Everything is going to be alright."

I began spilling out to Grandpa what I had dreamed. "I saw Mamma and Daddy. Daddy said he was proud of me. Mamma said she was sorry she isn't with me, but she is glad I'm with you Grandpa."

Grandpa held me, reassuring me everything would be just fine.

Suddenly, we heard a bunch of commotion. The men were struggling to bring a big man through the front door. He had handcuffs on, but that didn't stop him from putting up a big fight. He was a big, burly bear of a man. He looked like a mad grizzly. He was saying something about a "Sorry-ass bastard" that had beat and impregnated his daughter. He said he wanted the bastard to suffer at his own hands.

I had never in my life seen anyone so mad. It took all the men to bring him in and lock him up. It took a while, but they finally managed to get him in the cell. Then he started throwing the cot and side table against the wall.

Suddenly, I heard a woman's voice crying, "Papa, stop!"

Evie

"I won't stop until that no-good bastard is dead. Where in the hell is he? You said he was in custody," the irate man demanded.

Dullie shouted back, "He ain't here! They took him to the State Prison. Stop yer yellin'. Don't worry, he won't be havin' a picnic over there. He'll get what's coming to him."

The woman began crying harder.

Dullie looked at us and explained what he had gathered about the woman. He said that Al Jenkins had took up with the young woman. He had met her a couple of towns south of here and brought her back to live with him. I bet he had promised her the world; turned out he used her for a maid, among other things. The pitiful girl turned up pregnant. This had made Jenkins mad and he beat her up pretty bad. Her Daddy got wind of it.

"He held up at your folk's place waiting on Jenkins," Dullie explained. "When ya'll pulled up into the yard. he thought you was Jenkins and shot at you. I tried to talk some sense into him. I told him Jenkins would probably never see the light of day. I explained what all Jenkins is accused of, and that he is getting ready to stand trial for murder. This made Clayton Collins, even madder; he wants to kill Jenkins with his bare hands."

I looked over at the furious man and noticed he had calmed down some. His hands were bleeding from hitting everything. Dullie tossed him a wet towel to clean up with. I noticed Josh had not yet showed up at the jailhouse; this was not like Josh. He would have come back to me right away.

"Where is Josh" I asked.

Dullie didn't answer me.

"Dullie?" I pressed him.

With a strange look on his face, Dullie said, "Well, I was about to get to that." He paused as if he was trying to figure out how to tell me something.

I jumped up, feeling a terrible trepidation. "Josh is hurt, isn't he?" I cried.

Grandpa looked from me to Dullie and then back at me.

"Now, Evelyn don't panic. I'm sure he'll be walking in the door any minute," Grandpa said, trying to comfort me.

Dullie walked over to us, put his hands in his pockets, and said, "Well, the truth is he won't be walking in the door. Not for a while anyway."

"Dullie what are you saying?" I screamed.

Dullie straddled an old-wooded chair; he rubbed his hand over his face and paused like he was trying to figure out how to tell me something.

Evie

"Josh insisted on going into the house first," Dullie began. "Mr. Grizzly over there didn't know Jenkins from Adam. He thought Josh was Jenkins and laid right into him."

I heard myself scream "No!"

"We stopped him from killing your man, but he ain't in good shape. I'm sorry," Dullie said, and looked like he meant it. "He'll be laid up in the hospital for a while. He looks to have a broken nose, maybe a few cracked ribs, but he will mend."

I couldn't believe Dullie's words. I ran out the door without thinking; my only thoughts were to get to Josh. I felt such guilt that he was hurt while trying to protect me and what was mine. Grandpa followed me, yelling for me to stop. Poker was running alongside Grandpa, barking.

I held up for a moment. "Grandpa, I have to see Josh!"

"It's near midnight!" he said, breathing hard from running. "I'm going with you!"

It comforted me to know that Grandpa would come with me. We set off together at a quick pace.

When we got to the doors of the hospital, a "night watchman" was there. He said he wasn't allowed to let anyone in unless they were kin. I flat-out lied for the first time in my life.

"Joshua Harrison is my husband and he's been hurt," I said.

"This here is Joshua's Grandpa," I said, pointing to Grandpa.

The night watchman looked from me to Grandpa and back again to me. He looked like he was having a hard time trying to decide if I was telling the truth.

"Please, sir, I must get to my husband quickly!" I pled.

My urgency must have convinced him; he stepped aside. Grandpa quickly opened the door and we stepped into the hospital.

I said to Grandpa, "I'm sorry for lying."

"I know you don't make a habit of lying; it would be different if you did," Grandpa assured me. "Just find your man and don't worry about it."

As we walked down the hall, we came face to face with a giant nurse.

"How in God's green earth did you people get in here?" she asked with a big, gravelly voice.

"Joshua Harris is my husband, and he is hurt. I need to get to him! He needs me!" I desperately said to her.

The nurse was not convinced. She responded, "Oh, yeah? Where's your wedding ring? Mr. Harris' records show that he is single. Just turn around and go back the way you came in."

Evie

I had no choice but to run past her. I looked in every room until I finally found Josh.

I walked into the room and was shocked when I saw Josh. His face was swollen twice the normal size. My heart fell at the sight of him.

Dr. Hamilton was still working on him. The doctor greeted me with a tired look.

"He took quite a beating," Dr. Hamilton said.

I nodded in agreement, tears on the edge of my eyes.

"Joshua" I whispered.

"He won't be able to respond for a while. I gave him medication to put him out. He was in a lot of pain, the doctor explained.

"What all is wrong with him, doctor?" I asked, afraid to know.

To my surprise, Dr. Hamilton began listing his injuries. "He has a broken nose, split lip, a broken wrist, and three cracked ribs."

I sat down in the chair next to Josh and began to cry.

"I'm sorry, Josh. I'm so sorry."

Suddenly, Grandpa came running into the room. He was being chased by the giant nurse. Her big, gravelly voice began shouting orders for us to leave. Dr. Hamilton raised his hand to quiet her.

"It is alright, Nurse Wagner, they'll be leaving soon."

The nurse left shaking her head in aggravation. Grandpa sat in a chair in the far corner of the room.

We all sat silent for a few moments. Dr. Hamilton broke the silence.

"Congratulations on the outcome of your trial, Evelyn. I wish we would have all known early on what we know now. Al Jenkins sure had us all fooled."

Dr. Hamilton looked right at me for a moment and then said; "I would like to ask your forgiveness, Evelyn."

I looked right back at Dr. Hamilton with tears in my eyes. We both knew what he was talking about: Mama had gone to Dr. Hamilton in confidence. She confided in him about the beatings from Al Jenkins. Dr Hamilton then confronted Jenkins, causing everything to get much worse.

Evelyn, there isn't a day that goes by that I don't regret confronting Jenkins. I was angry. I wanted answers from Jenkins as to why your mother had bruises. Jenkins, being the snake and con artist that he is, convinced me it wasn't him but Laura who was abusing herself. I knew your mother hadn't been herself; things weren't adding up. I actually showed up at your home on an unexpected social call to see if I could discover some wrongdoing. Jenkins met me at the door and told me my timing was impeccable. He said he was calling me when I showed up at the door. He said your mother had fallen and hit her head. I walked into the bedroom, shocked to discover your mother was dead. I examined her; I could tell her wounds were more severe than wounds caused by a mere fall. I began to question Jenkins. He knew I was suspicious and that I questioned his explanation of what happen. That was when you walked into the house. I'm ridden with guilt, Evelyn. I should have listened more closely and believed your mother when she first came to me. I should not have betrayed her trust."

Tears were flowing down my cheeks just thinking of Mama and what she must have gone through.

Grandpa wanting to rescue me from my sadness. He spoke and said, "Yes, you should have listened, but what's done is done now. Let's all move forward. Come, Evie, I'm taking you home."

We left the hospital and found Poker was waiting for us outside the doors. His tail wagged back and forth; he seemed relieved to see us.

"Thanks for waiting on us, Poker, and putting up with this crazy long day we all have had," Grandpa said as he rubbed Poker's head.

We walked back to Grandpa's truck with heavy hearts. both wondering the same thing: would Mama still be here if

Dr. Hamilton had believed Mama and not listened to Evil Al's lies?

It was now one in the morning. Grandpa and I were both plum wore out. After discussing it, we decided we needed a good night sleep before we could face going back to the house. Grandpa rented us a hotel room. I crawled into the bed and looked over at Grandpa; he was sound asleep. It didn't take more than two minutes to fall asleep. I thought I would fall asleep right away, considering how tired I was, but instead I tossed and turned for hours. I had so looked forward to finally sleeping in my own bed, but after learning Evil Al had a "strange woman" in the house, I didn't feel so eager anymore.

I also wondered if all that fighting with the grizzly man happened inside the house; hopefully, they all had sense enough to go outside. I could just imagine a bunch of blood stains all over the pretty lace curtains. I feared what I would see when I walked into the house tomorrow. I so wanted it to be just the way Mama had left it. Laying here thinking on all this made me recall Al Jenkins' women companion. She really wasn't a woman at all; she looked to be just a young girl, maybe just a little older than me, and she was pretty.

I couldn't help but wonder what in the world she was doing with that beady-eyed, greasy-haired Al Jenkins. I then remembered the look in her eyes; our eyes had met as I was

Evie

leaving the jailhouse. She was sitting in the chair by the door. I noticed her belly stuck out, but not too much. She was probably only a few months pregnant. There was a deep sadness in her eyes. It dawned on me she wasn't with Al Jenkins by choice; that evil monster had forced her to be with him.

I bet he threatened her. I thought. *I would bet my life on it. I will get to the bottom of this, I will see if my hunches are right. Evil Al, may you rot in hell.*

I felt justified in thinking those thoughts. I would never wish that on any soul on earth except Evil Al.

I finally closed my eyes and fell into a fitful sleep.

I awakened to Poker licking my face.

"I thought you would never wake up, girl. I had to go get Poker to do help you out of your deep slumber," Grandpa said with a smile on his face.

"Grandpa, how did you get Poker in the hotel?"

"Easy, we just walked right on in. We just had to wait for the clerk to have his backed turned, that's all."

"How are we going to get him out of here?"

"I don't rightly know," Grandpa answered. I thought I would let you figure that out, little Missy."

I laughed.

Chapter 27

Surprisingly Grandpa, Poker, and I were able to escape with only a head shake and a finger wag from the hotel clerk.

We were once again headed to my childhood home. Grandpa and I were both quiet and lost in our own thoughts on the way there. I just couldn't get the grizzly man's daughter out of my mind. Grandpa was probably thinking on how he needed to get his broken window fixed. The cold morning air was blowing into the truck. He was swearing under his breath about the busted-out windows.

We carefully drove up into the yard.

"Place looks to be in pretty good shape. I couldn't see much of it the other night; it was so dark," Grandpa said out loud, more to himself than to me.

I didn't bring up Evil Al manipulating the men in the church to fix the place up, but I couldn't help remembering.

I noticed splatters of blood on the walkway. I felt sad knowing it was probably Josh's blood.

"Thank you, Josh, for risking your life to save what was mine," I whispered—although I wish he hadn't tried to be so brave. Maybe then he would be by my side instead of laid up in a hospital bed.

Grandpa overheard me and said, "Don't worry, Evie, he is young and will mend just fine; you can tend to him later but right now you need to get acquainted with your home again."

We walked into the front door/ I was surprised and delighted to see everything clean and in place. It looked as clean as Mama had always kept it. It appeared everything had recently been freshly polished and dusted.

"Well, the house seems to be good and clean," Grandpa commented.

I shook my head in agreement as I looked in every room. Poker was right alongside me sniffing every corner. I looked in my room; this appeared to be where the girl had slept. In my closet there were three worn but neatly pressed dresses. She had a pair of worn dress shoes on the floor of the closet. A Bible and some story books were stacked on the dresser. The items this girl owned did not look like those of a girl with ill morals. She even owned a well-worn Bible. This girl was a mystery.

I continued to look around. I opened my dresser drawers and noticed her undergarments were also worn but neatly folded. I opened the second drawer; she had two sweaters and socks in this drawer. I saw something else something that appeared to be a book. I picked it up and opened it; it was a journal. I quickly skimmed over it. The girl seemed to be expressing her feelings in the journal. I felt this journal probably might solve some mysteries surrounding this girl. Each day was dated; she even put the time of each entry. The girl's daddy may have called her a tramp, but she appeared to be a very neat clean and thoughtful girl.

Suddenly, Grandpa walked into the room, startling me. I felt ashamed for plundering through the girl's things.

"What you got there?" Grandpa asked.

"It looks to be the journal of the grizzly man's daughter," I answered, putting the journal back into the drawer. I began to explain to Grandpa my guilt over looking through the strange girl's things when suddenly Poker interrupted with a loud bark and growl. We ran out of the room to figure out what was causing him to make such a ruckus.

We found Poker in Mama's bedroom growling at the armoire. I opened the armoire. Evil Al's clothes were hanging in it, along with many of his other possessions.

"I reckon a dog can smell rotten character even from their clothes," Grandpa said.

"I'm getting rid of everything that even has a hint of Al Jenkins attached to it," I declared as I shut the armoire door. But that was a task I wasn't ready to tackle right at that moment.

"It's ok, Poker, it's just a bunch of clothes and shoes," I said. I turned to go into the kitchen to find Grandpa and me something to eat.

But there was no convincing Poker that everything was ok. He continued to growl at the armoire, except now he was growling even louder.

Grandpa suddenly looked very serious. "Hmmm. Poker is a smart dog. He would not keep growling at mere clothes. We better take a better look inside that armoire again."

Grandpa slowly opened the doors of the armoire, Daddy's prized possession, which had been handed down the family line. Daddy said it had arrived here on a ship with our kin over one hundred years ago.

How dare Evil Al take ownership like it was his own.

Grandpa spread the clothes apart so we could see into the armoire. Poker growled and lunged inside; suddenly, a figure sprang out.

It was the grizzly man's daughter!

Poker bit down and caught her dress between his teeth. He growled loudly. She tried to run but she fell to the floor instead.

"Please don't hurt me! Don't kill me!" the frightened girl cried.

"Poker, let go!" Grandpa demanded as he grabbed Poker's collar.

The girl slipped back. She was lying on the ground, looking like a frightened animal caught in a trap. She glared at Grandpa and me with fear in her eyes. Grandpa pulled Poker, who was still growling and arching to get the girl, by the collar and shoved him out the back door. This seemed to relieve the girl a little; she sat up and looked less frightened. Grandpa walked back into the bedroom. We all stared at each other for a time.

Grandpa broke the silence. "What in world were you doing, held up there in the armoire?"

The girl was huddled in a tight ball. She whispered something, but we could not hear her.

"You're going to have to speak up some, young lady," Grandpa ordered." We can't hear a word you're saying."

"I was hiding," the girl said faintly.

"Well, that wasn't a mystery," Grandpa answered, almost seeming amused. He turned serious. "We want some answers. We aren't planning on harming you. Looks to me like harm has already been done to you. You look scrawny, like you haven't had enough to eat. You're as scared as a jack rabbit, and you have a young'un on the way that I betcha you weren't counting on."

Surprisingly, it seemed Grandpa's words relaxed the girl a little.

She sat up and said, "I thought you were going to kill me."

I helped the girl off the floor, reassuring her we would not hurt her. The girl sighed with relief. Her whole body was shaking. I led her into the kitchen and guided her to the kitchen chair. Grandpa went to the back door; he let Poker back, in demanding he behave. Poker ran right over to the girl and sniffed her. He was no longer growling, but he was not happy with our intruder. His tail stayed between his legs in protest.

I gave the girl water and sat in the chair next to her. Grandpa also sat at the table; he motioned for Poker to lie down. The girl took a sip of water and looked down at her hands in her lap. I found myself feeling compassion for this girl; it would be awful to be in her position. In the past few years, I'd been in some pretty awful predicaments myself. At least I was never carrying a baby; I could be thankful for that. I figured the best way to be was understanding.

"How long have you been living here?" I asked.

"Five months and four days, ma'am," the girl answered, her voice barely above a whisper.

"Well," I said as I looked around, "I want to thank you for keeping this place so nice and neat.

She looked at me with a puzzled look on her face and asked, "Is this your home?"

"Yes…well, it belonged to my Mama and Daddy, but they are dead. They left the house and property to me."

The girl looked puzzled again. "But I thought Alexander…" The girl didn't finish her sentence. She stood up. "I'm sorry. I guess I don't belong here. I'll get my things and leave."

"Wait, where will go?" I asked.

The girl looked down "I don't know."

"I saw you in the jailhouse. I heard your Daddy doesn't welcome you home anymore. Is that true?"

The girl nodded.

"Since he is in jail right now, could you go home?"

"My father got released. His brother bailed him out. He warned me not to set foot on his property," the girl answered sadly. "I walked here from town last night. I didn't realize Alexander did not own this house; he told me this was his home. I thought I could stay here a while until I figured out what to do. I was planning on leaving before Alexander got released."

"So, you want to be away from him?" I asked.

Before the girl could answer, Grandpa spoke up and said, "I'm going to ask you a question out right, if you don't mind." He didn't wait for a response. "Are you really Al Jenkins' girl? Did you really choose to be with that snake of a man?"

The girl looked down and shook her head no. "I did not choose to be with him."

I suddenly felt very sorry for this girl; she was yet another one of Evil Al's victims. I wanted her to trust us. I grabbed her by the hands and looked her square in the face and said, "Al Jenkins has hurt a lot of people. He has especially hurt my family. He is in jail and cannot hurt any of us anymore."

The girl looked relieved, yet sad, she began telling us about herself.

"It was just Daddy and me. Mama died of pneumonia about four years ago. Last spring, Daddy broke his leg trimming a fallen tree limb; it was hard for him to get around; he wasn't able to work much. In the town paper, I noticed a request for a housekeeper and cook a few towns away. I phoned Al Jenkins right away. We met at the town diner. He asked me what my experience was in cooking and cleaning. I told him I had been doing both for years. He offered me the job and a salary I never even imagined. I figured it would help pay our bills, at least until my father's leg healed. At the time, Mr. Jenkins seemed so kind. He told me he was a widower. He explained that, because he was a servant of God, he didn't have time to clean the house or cook meals. He said it would be better for him if I were a live-in housekeeper; he would make it worthwhile to me in a generous salary."

Grandpa couldn't help voicing his distain. "That snake in the grass. He should be strung up by his legs and left in the sun to wither."

The girl continued, "I didn't feel comfortable doing this, but he seemed so kind and genuine I told him I would try it out for a time. I knew my father would not agree to this, so I stretched the truth a little by telling him that Al Jenkins was an feeble old man that needed help. Father reluctantly agreed but insisted on meeting him. I made excuses every time my father wanted to meet him. I know it was wrong, but we were desperate; we already had our electricity turned off and we could barely buy food. We were in danger of losing our home. At first. living here seemed to work out. I was able to give my father money and we got caught up on our bills. Then father's leg got better. He started getting more work. He asked me to quit and come back home. He said he would rather have me home keeping my own house, and that that old man Jenkins needed to find another housekeeper. I expressed this to Mr. Jenkins, and that's when it happened."

The girl's eyes suddenly filled with tears.

"What happened" I asked.

"He changed," the girl whispered.

Grandpa and I both knew what she meant. Al Jenkins became angry when things were no longer going his way. Al Jenkins suddenly became Evil Al Jenkins. The girl didn't even have to explain; we realized this was probably the day this poor girl's body was compromised. She did explain, however, that Evil Al threatened her and her father if she were ever to leave, so she kept giving her father excuses about why she wasn't coming home just yet. The girl looked so frightened, remembering all she had gone through.

I asked her what her name was.

"Susan," she answered.

"Susan, you don't have to continue talking; I know it's hard to recall painful memories."

"It's ok. If you don't mind, I would like to continue. It feels good to have someone listen who understands and cares."

I nodded.

"When I discovered I was pregnant, I told Alexander." She paused. "Alexander is the name he made me call him. The pregnancy made him angry: he beat me so bad I thought he would kill me and my unborn child. I was praying so hard to be spared."

Hearing her say these things brought tears to my eyes.

"He told me I needed to do something to 'get rid of this kid.' If I didn't do something, he would. Then he laughed and said he had a trial to attend. He said he would enjoy seeing a little brat he once knew get what was coming to her. I know now he was talking about you. When he left, I knew this was my chance to get away. I knew he would try to kill me whether I stayed or not. I made it to my father's. I ran into the house. Father saw me all bruised and beaten. I cried and told him everything. Father was so furious, he shouted, 'I'm going to kill him!' Father got his gun. I pleaded for him not to go; I was afraid Father would be killed. He pushed me aside and said I had lied to him, and that I was not innocent in all this. He said he was going to Jenkins' house to wait for him. He was going to give him what was coming to him."

"It was your daddy who shot at us," Grandpa piped in.

"I know. I'm so sorry. You could have been killed," Susan said with a shaky voice.

Evie

I felt great compassion for Susan. In many ways, our lives were similar. We were about the same age. We had both lost our mothers. Al Jenkins had robbed from both of us. Although he hadn't been successful in defiling me, it wasn't because he didn't try. I could have been in the same shameful predicament that Susan was in. I could not place judgment upon her.

"Susan, I need to speak to my grandpa alone."

Susan nodded and rose out of the chair to leave us alone.

"Please stay here, Susan. Grandpa and I will step outside."

When we were outside the door, Grandpa said, "You don't even have to ask. The poor girl needs a place to stay. No sense kicking her out, especially in her tender condition."

So, it was decided Susan would stay with us, for the time being at least. Susan was incredibly relieved and thankful. She cried and hugged us both many times.

She kept saying, "I didn't know where to go. I had nowhere else."

"Don't worry. Your place is with us right now," I assured her.

Grandpa insisted on sleeping on the sofa in the sitting room. I would take over Mama and Daddy's room and Susan would continue sleeping in my room. Susan was very grateful and insisted on continuing with the housecleaning and cooking. She said she wanted to earn her keep. Grandpa spent much of his time tending to the outside of the house. Winter was coming; he wanted to make sure everything was in order before he left to return to his home in Illinois. I didn't want Grandpa to leave; he had no family in Trenton. I felt his place is with me. I would approach him on this matter later; right now, my thoughts and concerns were with Josh. It was a good thing Susan would continue keeping the house in order because, I planned on spending my time at the hospital helping Josh regain his health.

Josh spent a whole week in the hospital. When he was released, he still needed much recovery time. With his family's blessings, I continued nursing Josh back to health. I explained to him about Susan and how we had invited her to live with us as long as she needed to. He shook his head and said he hoped I was doing the right thing. I assured him I was; I told him it felt right in my heart, and that's what mattered.

Two weeks went by since Josh was released from the hospital. He was almost back to normal. Surprisingly, Dullie hired Josh back on staff to be the head deputy. Dullie explained that the town was now a two-deputy town. He said that he,

Evie

along with many of the townspeople, were impressed at Josh's bravery. In my opinion, I think Dullie felt pressure from some important men in town to hire Josh back. Whatever the reason, I was grateful Josh had his old job back. I felt responsible for him losing it in the first place. Josh told Dullie he would be honored to have his job back under one condition.

"What would that be?" Dullie asked.

"I want you to stay out of my business, Dullie," Josh stated flatly.

"That will be no problem. I don't like your business anyhow," Dullie answered back with a *hummph*.

Josh and the other deputy, Tim, became fast friends. Josh explained to me that Tim was the deceased Smiths' nephew. He had inherited their place and decided to call it home. Suddenly, I felt sad; the memory of the Smiths brought tears to my eyes. Josh saw the change in my countenance and apologized for bringing up sad memories.

"It's okay," I assured Josh. "The Smiths were such wonderful people."

"Yeah, Tim was real surprised they left the place to him. I guess it makes sense because they never had children of their own."

261

I didn't remind Josh that they actually did have a son who died at age twelve. I will be forever grateful for his clothes.

I tried my best to get Grandpa and Poker to stay. He said he would be back; he had to settles things at home. He insisted I accept a little money from him to keep bills paid while we figured out a way for me to make a living. Money had been earned from crops, but Al Jenkins had the money in his bank account. Steve Harrison said he would work hard at restoring what was rightfully mine, but it could take months.

So, I did what I knew best: I prayed, "Lord, please help me figure out how to make a living."

As I watched Grandpa and Poker drive down the road, I felt a sad emptiness. I prayed it wouldn't be long before they returned. I have grown close to Grandpa. I even thought to call him "Grandpa-Daddy," but I figured it would be too confusing, and besides that would require a lot of explaining. In my heart, he was becoming almost as special to me as Daddy was. I could tell he hated to leave me too. He had tears in his eyes. He told me since I was almost grown, that I could very well be trusted to be on my own for a spell. He mentioned he had a long talk with Josh. He felt Josh was a good man and would respect and look out for me. He went on to say he would be back before too long. God had given him a gift and didn't want to lose this gift again. I walked back in the house with a heavy heart, but I felt great joy and love that Grandpa would call me a "gift."

Susan was sitting at the kitchen table, dabbing her eyes.

I sat down with her. "What is wrong Susan, why are you crying?"

"I'm sad to see your grandpa and Poker leave."

It warmed my heart to see how attached Susan had become to Grandpa. However, it did not surprise me. Grandpa accepted Susan just as she is: this is just what Susan needed. He also gave her advice on life. He told her she had to forgive herself and move on from the past. Living and regretting the past would only hinder her future. After several of these conversations, Susan's depression lifted and she began talking about the future with her child.

Chapter 28

As weeks went by, my money started running out. Susan and I needed to figure out a way to earn a living. We tried to make our money last as long as we could. We ate beans and cornbread almost every night; we didn't turn the lights on unless we really needed to; and we tried not to use much water. We put our money together: between us we had $143.17. This would not last long. We wondered if any of the women in town needed housecleaning done. We drew up notices and posted them all over town. A week went by with no calls. A second week went by, still no calls. We figured since times were so hard, women were cleaning their own houses; even the uppity ladies on the west end of town must have been cleaning their own houses.

As the days went by, we got more and more discouraged. One day, I found Susan sitting on the front steps crying; she was worried she would not be able to keep her baby if she couldn't provide. I inwardly wondered if I would be able to keep the farmhouse. I sat down next to Susan. I told her how

Evie

Mama used to say, "If you didn't know what to do, pray." So, we sat there on the steps and prayed I would not lose the farmhouse. We also prayed Susan would always be able to cloth and feed her child. We had no more finished our prayer when the phone rang; it was Josh asking if he could come over for a visit. He wanted to bring Tim. He said Tim had been lonesome lately. I realized right away what Josh was getting at; he was hinting for dinner.

I said, "Yes, of course you can come for a visit. Susan and I can fix you boys some dinner if you would like."

"I thought you would never ask. How about six o'clock?" Josh asked with excitement in his voice.

"Six would be fine," I answered.

It had been a good long while since I had seen Josh. I'm ashamed to say it had a lot to do with money. I only had a few dollars to my name. I needed to make the gasoline in the truck last. If I had invited him to come see me, then I would have to fix him a meal. Meal fixin's are pretty slim right now. Josh went and invited himself. Now me and Susan needed to come up with a meal for the boys. We decided to kill and fry one of our few chickens. We had four potatoes left in the root cellar. We could cream those. All we needed to come up with was dessert.

Most men liked something sweet after a meal. I knew daddy did. Mama could bake the best peach cobbler a person ever tasted. It made my mouth water just thinking about it. The only thing we really had to make a dessert out of were the apples from the apple tree in the back of the house. Trouble was the apples were full of worms. Daddy always kept it sprayed free of worms, of course, but Evil Al didn't have sense enough to do that. We decided to pick the apples from the tree anyway. We would never tell the boys, but we cut the apples up and pulled the worms out the best we could. We cooked the apples and made fried apple pies out of them.

We figured a little worm never hurt anyone.

The boys loved the dinner. They especially liked the warm apple pies. As they ate the pies, we couldn't help but snicker. The boys asked us what was funny. We told them we were happy to see them. We had fried up about six little pies; before the evening, was over the boys had eaten everything. They said the pies were about the best thing they had ever eaten. An idea flashed across my mind. When the boys left, I mentioned my idea to Susan.

"Susan, why don't we start our own business selling pies. Everyone likes pies. A person would use their last dollar to get a good piece of pie."

Susan smiled at me, touched her growing belly, and said, "Well, it's worth a try."

That night, as I lay in bed, I thought how God sure works in mysterious ways. He gave me the most unlikely friend. We both needed each other. Circumstances brought us together. Fate made us friends.

We rose early the next morning and prayed the Lord would bless our new business. We knew we could not use the wormy apples, so we headed into town to buy a bushel from the grocer. As we drove down the road, we went past the Smith's old house, which was now Tim's house. We noticed Tim was in his front yard. We backed up and said hello.

"Hey, where are you girls headed in such a hurry?" Tim asked with a big smile on his face."

"We going to Pete's Grocery to buy a bushel of apples," I answered.

"Don't waste your money," Tim said. "I have two apple trees in the back yard plum full of apples. You girls are welcome to as many as you would like."

As Tim was offering the apples, I remembered the slice of apple pie I ate when I was at the Smiths'. The apples were sweet and delicious. Susan and I jumped out of the car and ran to the backyard. It was as if gold hung from the branches.

Tim noticed our excitement and said, "Take 'em all. They'll just fall to the ground and rot because I can't eat all."

We borrowed every sack and bucket we could find around his house and loaded them all up with our delicious, sweet, edible gold. As we picked apples, I noticed there were berries on vines along the fence. I mentioned the berries; Tim did not even notice the berry-vine along the fence.

I asked if I could pick the berries.

"Help yourself," he said. "I'd just as soon you had them then the birds get 'em."

Tim looked puzzled and asked, "What are ya'll planning to do with all the fruit? I know you two 'pint-sized' girl's ain't going eat all this. I mean, I know Susan is eaten for two, but ya'll picked enough to feed a good size army."

Susan stood in front of Tim and said, "Because of your good nature, and sharing your apples and berries, Evie and me will have a good start to our new business of pie-making. I want you to know you can have as many free pies as you want, since you give us all these fixin's."

Susan smiled her pretty smile and Tim looked real flushed. The attraction between these two was so strong I had to look away.

Chapter 29

Susan and I spent hours peeling and slicing apples. We sliced apple pieces real thin to dry in the sunshine. We would use these for fried apple pies. We also canned apples. I was so grateful for all the jars Mama had stored in the cellar. We used the rest of the apples for pies. We fried up thirty apple pies and baked fifteen apple and ten berry pies. We loaded up the pies in daddy's old truck and headed into town. Our first stop was Anne's Café.

We walked in carrying pies. We were turned down flat.

"We bake our own pies here," the chef said. "Don't need anymore. Ain't sellin what we got."

Discouraged, we left the café with the pies in our hands. I was looking down at my pies in my hands, trying to be careful and not drop them, and I ran right smack into Josh's Daddy, the governor. The three pies I was balancing crashed to the ground with a sickening thud. The delicious syrupy apples were now mixed with dirt and gravel.

"Oh, I'm so sorry," I muttered as I crouched down to pick up the gooey mess.

"Nonsense! I need to apologize to you; it seemed I wasn't watching where I was going," Mr. Harrison said. "Here, allowing me to pay for those pies you just purchased."

"No need, Mr. Harrison."

"I insist."

"Well, you see, Mr. Harrison, I didn't actually purchase these pies. I brought them into town to sell them. Susan and I had the idea of starting a business making and selling pies. I guess it wasn't a good idea after all."

"Why do you say that, Miss Evie?" Mr. Harrison asked with real concern in his eyes.

"I tried to sell them at Anne's Café. It seems they already have enough pies. Trouble is, I have a bunch more in Daddy's truck."

Mr. Harrison asked me how much I wanted for each pie.

"I was hoping to get seventy-five cents a pie."

"How many pies do you have there? It looks to me like you have six. According to my calculations, I owe you four dollars and fifty cents. Now hand me my pies."

We handed the pies to Mr. Harrison. He walked right into the Corner Café. A few moments later, he came out of the café with a big smile on his face and no pies. He said he sold every pie for eighty cents each. I asked how he did it, knowing he probably sold them because he was an important man.

"It was easy," Mr. Harrison said. "I told them my son has never bragged on anything as much as he has these pies."

Mr. Harrison looked over at the truck and noticed our other pies.

"Looks like we have more money to make," he said with a wide smile. We went all around town, and the surrounding towns, and sold every pie. We thanked Mr. Harrison many times over. We were so thankful for his help.

He held up his hand and said, "Ladies no need to thank me. I thank you. I was wondering what type of business to invest in; I believe I found it. I want you to think of a catchy name for your pies. I will do the rest."

Susan and I could not get over our good fortune. We decided to celebrate that night by having the boys over for roast beef and potatoes. We used some of the earnings from the pies to buy the beef, a luxury we had not enjoyed in a long time. After dinner, we all put our brains together to come up with a name for our pies. We decided to put both our Mamas' names together and call them Laura-Kay pies. We ended the evening with the best-tasting dessert my taste buds had ever experience: a pie made from a blend of fresh plump plums and strawberries with a rich cream sauce.

Life took on a certain routine. Susan and I worked hard at baking pies. We were up to fourteen different varieties. We had restaurants ordering pies as far away as Jackson. Thankfully, we found a way to make a living. We could keep the farm running, lights on, and food on the table. I had a feeling of real satisfaction deep inside. I felt Mama and Daddy would be proud of me. This made me smile. I found myself singing and smiling a lot more these days.

Susan was smiling a lot more too. Tim had officially asked her to court him. He said he was sorry she didn't have the father of her baby around, but he supposed she had good reason for it, and he would respect that. She told him she was really glad the baby's father wasn't anywhere near. She figured this was as good a time as any to tell him the ugly truth. If he would hate her and leave her for what had happened in the past, better it happen before the baby was born.

She told him everything, how her father was hurt and couldn't work and how she answered an ad in the paper looking for a live-in housekeeper position. She took the job out of desperation and was manipulated and finally raped by Al Jenkins. Tim got angry, not with her, but at Jenkins. He said never in his life had he felt like killing a man, but he wanted to kill Jenkins. Josh calmed Tim down and assured him Jenkins was getting what he deserved. Tim finally came to terms with things and told Susan he felt honor to pick up the beautiful pieces Al Jenkins had left behind. Susan was filled with joy. She said she never thought a good man would ever lay eyes on her again. God sent a wonderful man that accepted her at her worst: pregnant with another man's baby.

The elders of the church paid us a visit one day. When I saw them approach, I was glad Susan was in town because I figured the visit had to do with her being pregnant and all. The town had been without a preacher since Al Jenkins went to prison. They had a guest speaker ever since. I have gone every Sunday. I even got Susan to go with me a few times. Sadly, the stares and cruel words from the ladies of the church had kept her away. I got stares and cruel words too sometimes; I felt the ladies of the church thought I had a contagious disease because they never sat near me, but I keep going because it would make Mama happy.

She would say, "We don't go to church for the people. We go for God."

She would also tell me to forgive the ladies of the church, for they know not what they were doing. Mama was a much better person than I, because I think they know full well what they were doing. I opened the door and let the two elders in. I offered them pie, expecting them to say no, but they accepted my offer with smile and a "Thank you." They sat eating pie and making small talk.

Finally, I flat-out asked "Gentlemen, may I ask the reason for your visit?"

"Oh yes, Evie. We came to find out how we could get in touch with Brother John Sanders. We were very impressed with Brother John when he visited here. We would like to approach him with the possibility of taking over as pastor of the church."

I could not believe my ears! How wonderful it would be if Brother John and Beth could live near me.

I gave them Brother John's address. "Thank you kindly, Miss Evie, for the information and for delicious cherry pie. I won't tell the missus, but I believe your pie is the best cherry pie I've ever eaten."

"Thank you for your kind words, gentlemen. I will pass the compliment on to Susan."

"Oh yes, we need to thank you for reaching out and taking in that unfortunate soul."

"Gentlemen, you are welcome for the information and the pie, but you are not welcome for the last compliment you paid me."

"Miss Evie, surely you are not taking offence; this women's own father won't have anything to do with her. She is a harlot. She soiled herself with an older man, enough to get impregnated by him. Please tell us she did not bake the pie we just ate, for I fear I may vomit."

I felt the heat rise up on my neck; I wanted so badly to scream at them to "Get out!" But I knew I had to control my temper, lest they would go around the town spreading ill words about me as well.

"Gentlemen," I said, collecting myself. "Susan is not an unfortunate soul. The thing that is unfortunate is having a father who doesn't even realize his only daughter sacrificed her safety to provide food on the table when he could not. When she was in trouble, he threw her in the streets. No, she isn't the unfortunate soul; her father and her abuser and all those who speak against her are the unfortunate ones. Good day, gentlemen!"

"Ah, ah, good day," the two men said, walking away quickly without looking back.

Josh came to visit. We decided to sit on the front porch. As we sat on the porch, looking out across the front yard, both deep in our own thoughts, Josh reminded me that Al Jenkins' trial was coming up soon. Josh's brother Steven had such an interest in the case he was helping the defense attorney come up with evidence. He said they had a lot of evidence, but they would like even more to guarantee Jenkins never went free.

Josh said that Jenkins was being a sly con artist even behind prison walls; he had a lawyer convinced of his innocence. Just the thought of Jenkins going free sent chills up my spine.

I suppose I looked worried. Josh put his arms around me and said, "Don't worry Evie. Truth rises to the top. Evil never wins."

I shook my head in agreement, but inwardly I feared that Jenkins would once again get his way.

Chapter 30

*L*ately, it was getting harder for Susan to stand while baking pies; her pregnant belly was huge. She had to sit to roll out the dough. It was exciting when the baby moved; Susan placed my hand on her belly. I felt a connection with the baby. Susan asked if I would mind if the baby called me Aunt Evie. Of course, I felt honored. I asked Susan when she thought the baby would arrive. She said she wasn't sure, but from the looks of her it would be sometime real soon. I helped Susan make baby clothes and diapers. She bought a used cradle that was advertised in the town paper and placed it beside her bed. All the handmade baby clothes were folded neatly in the second drawer of her dresser. We were ready for the baby.

A few days later, Susan was rolling pie dough while I was cutting up apples.

Suddenly, I heard Susan yell "What is happening?"

Susan had liquid pouring down her legs and onto the floor. It didn't take much sense to realize this had to do with birthing.

"Susan, I think the baby is fixin' to come!"

"Oh no! Oh no!" Susan cried.

"Did you think this baby was going to just stay inside you forever? I've never heard of a woman delivering a full-grown child."

Susan gave me a Look and I realized I'd better stop trying to be funny. Daddy was like that, always trying to be funny when nerve-wracking things were happening. I guess we were both nervous, because all of a sudden we just looked at each other and started giggling. I led her to the bedroom and helped her lie down. Then I got an old quilt and put it under the foot of the bed. I tried to get in touch with Dr. Hamilton; the nurse at the hospital said he was busy delivering a baby. The nurse said she would give him the message, and she advised us to come ahead to the hospital.

I walked back into the bedroom to tell Susan what I had found out. She had a tight grip on the headboard of the bed. She started hollering like a wounded animal. This scared me half to death, but I didn't tell Susan I was scared. I pretended to be brave and all; but on the inside, I was shaking something fierce.

"We need to go to the hospital" I shouted louder than I intended to.

"Can't!" Susan grimaced.

"What did you say?" I asked, knowing full well what she said.

"I can't walk," Susan explained.

Oh my! Oh my! Oh my! I began to panic in my mind. *What do I do? What do I do? I need to think! Think, think, think! What did the book say? Where is the book?*

I ran into the front room and grabbed the book. I quickly looked up delivery, page sixty-seven. I fumbled through the pages and finally found page sixty-seven.

Suddenly, I heard Susan scream my name.

"EVIE! EVIE!"

I dropped the book and took off running.

When I got to the bedroom, I took one look at Susan and instinct took over. I carefully helped her lay on the bed. I lifted her dress and removed her bloomers; this was no time for modesty. The baby's head was already showing about the size of a half dollar. I placed my hands down by the baby's head, ready to guide and hold the baby as it came through the birth canal. Susan screamed, then suddenly the baby then shot right out into my hands. I had to hold the baby tight to keep it from slipping from my grasp.

Oh no! It was still hooked on to Susan!

Suddenly, I heard the door open. It was Josh and Tim.

"Stay away!" I demanded, wanting to protect Susan's modesty.

"Is everything ok?" Josh asked from the front room.

I realized the baby wasn't crying. Instinct told me to clear the baby's mouth out. I rubbed the baby gently with a towel. The baby began to cry! Susan was trying to ask me a question. I realized I had not been listening I was so intent on holding on to the baby and helping it cry.

"Do I have a boy or a girl?" Susan demanded.

I hadn't even looked; I removed the towel from the baby.

"You have a boy!"

Susan was crying tears of joy as she reached for her baby boy. I handed the baby to Susan.

"I need to cut the umbilical cord," I said firmly.

"Don't hurt him," she pleaded.

"I won't."

I was nervous and unsure how to cut the cord. I poured alcohol over the knife and twine I had found earlier. With shaky hands, I tied the twine tightly around the cord about two inches from his naval and began cutting as Susan held her son tight. The cord was much tougher than I imagined. Finally, with great effort, I sawed through the cord and the baby was free!

Evie

Susan named her baby Paul Clayton Collins. She wanted to name her baby Paul because she liked reading about Paul in the Bible. "He had good character," she said. Clayton was her daddy's name. She loved her daddy even though he didn't want anything to do with her. She prayed someday his heart would soften. She wanted to be his daughter again. If it were me, I would just forget about the mean old fool, but who was I to judge Susan's heart?

I wanted to make Susan's heart happy, so the other day I asked Josh if he minded going over to Susan's daddy's place and explaining things to him. Her daddy needed to know his daughter was not a loose woman. She was taken against her will.

"Are you kidding me?" Josh protested. "That grizzly man almost did me in!"

"I know Josh, but Susan really misses her Daddy. He used to care for her, and since her baby doesn't have a real daddy to speak of, he needs a granddaddy."

"I'll think on it," Josh said as he took me into his arms, "but I'm not making any promises."

Our lives sure got busy after the birth of Paul. We took turns tending to him and baking pies. Of course, when he got hungry, I couldn't help much. Seems he was hungry all the time. He was a big baby: he would probably be a big man like his grandpa. He looked nothing like Al Jenkins, which was a mighty blessing from above.

I noticed Susan was having a hard time fitting her clothes and Paul's clothes in the little dresser in my old room. I figured there was no reason she couldn't use Daddy's chest of drawers. I would just remove daddy's belongings. As I opened the drawers, I realized Daddy's belongings were no longer in the drawers. These were Al Jenkins things!

I thought I had gotten rid of all his things when I emptied out Mama's armoire. I gathered up all his clothes from the first drawer, took them outside, and burned them. The second drawer appeared to have his undergarments in it. I did not want to touch them, so I went out on the back porch and found Mama's garden gloves. As I removed his garments, I noticed a black book on the bottom of the drawer. It appeared Al Jenkins keeps a journal.

As I opened and read it, my hands began to shake. I couldn't believe what I was reading. I had to stop reading because I was getting physically sick. Al Jenkins wrote in detail what he did to all his victims and how he killed them. The journal was full of written confessions. I had to get this book to the authorities. Al Jenkins' murder trial was coming up. If this didn't get him convicted, I didn't know what would!

Evie

As I walked out of the bedroom with the journal in my hand, I must have looked pretty upset because Susan wiped the dough from her hands, came over to me, and guided me to sit down in the kitchen chair.

"Evie, are you ok? You look as white as a sheet."

I handed her the journal. She opened it, after a moment she closed it shut.

"I have to take it to the authorities now," I informed her.

Susan looked away from me with tears in her eyes. "Evie, I wish you wouldn't."

"Why, Susan? This could be the evidence we need to put Al Jenkins away for good."

"He told me about the journal. He laughed and said he had written about me. Oh, Evie, he had me do some horrible things to myself and to him. If anyone were to read it, I would die of shame."

Susan was holding on to the journal so tightly her knuckles were white.

"Susan, find all those entries and tear them out. They will never be spoken of again. I swear to you." With shaky hands and tear-filled eyes, Susan searched the journal.

The pages were dated so she didn't have to read every filthy word. She began ripping pages out; there were twelve all

283

together. I lit a match at the kitchen sink and burned the pages. I looked at Susan. Shame and sadness filled her eyes.

"Susan, the past is the past. Let the memories burn up and be gone just like these pages."

With a quick knock, Josh let himself in.

"Evie! Evie!" he shouted.

"I'm right here, Josh," I said as I rinsed the last of the ashes down the sink.

"Al Jenkins is going to be set free! The stinking county judge doesn't think there is enough evidence for a trial. He threw out the case!"

I handed Josh the journal.

"There is enough evidence now."

"What's this?" Josh asked.

"Read it," I instructed.

Josh began flipping through the pages. His face turned bright red; his eyes filled with disbelief, then anger.

He grabbed my hand. "Come on. We have to take this in now!"

Susan had left the kitchen right after the last page was destroyed. She was holding Paul in the living room.

"Susan, we are taking the journal to the authorities. We need to get this to them before they free Jenkins," I said as we were running out the door.

Without looking up, Susan nodded in agreement.

I prayed on the way to town. "Lord, please let us get this journal into the right hands so Al Jenkins can stay behind bars where he belongs."

When we got to the jailhouse, Dullie and Tim looked mighty serious.

When Dullie saw us, he said, "Just the people I wanted to talk to. I have some news for you."

"What news?" I asked breathlessly.

"They've gone and let Jenkins free, and we hear he is headed this way. Word is, he told some of the guards he needed to reclaim some things that are rightfully his."

Dullie and Josh looked at each other and nodded wordlessly.

"We need to get you back home," Josh told me. He, Dullie, Tim, and I all piled into Daddy's truck.

"They could have given us more warning!" Josh said angrily.

"Yah, when a case is thrown out the prisoner is free to go!" Dullie said.

We raced back to the house as fast as we could go. I ran in and shouted for Susan.

The house was silent. We searched everywhere. Susan and the baby were nowhere to be found. All the contents in the chest of drawers were scattered over the floor. It looked as if Jenkins had been looking for his condemning journal.

The phone rang—I felt relief. Maybe this was Susan telling me she was at the neighbors.

I picked up the phone, "Susan!"

The voice on the other end sent chills up my spine.

"Well, Evelyn, isn't this a surprise? I bet you never thought you would have the honor of hearing my voice again!"

"Where is she?" I demanded, my voice shaking. "What have you done with Susan and the baby?"

"I haven't done anything with them…yet," the evil voice answered. There was a pause. I heard deep breathing. "I won't harm them if you do just as I say."

Josh, Dullie, and Tim were all asking me what was going on and who was I talking to. It was obvious I was upset. I could not help myself; I was shaking from head to toe. I quickly took the phone away from my ear and covered the mouthpiece.

"It's Al Jenkins. He is trying to blackmail me! My guess is he wants the journal."

Dullie quickly grabbed the phone from me. "Now listen here, Jenkins, this is the law. You better turn the girl and her child over to us right now, or you are going to end up back in the slammer!"

He fell silent. Al Jenkins was obviously telling his demands to Dullie. It seemed Dullie couldn't get a word in edgewise. Every time Dullie tried to say something he stopped in mid-sentence.

Jenkins must have hung up on Dullie, because Dullie slammed the phone down and swore under his breath.

"What did he say?" we all asked.

"Well, it seems Jenkins took the girl and her baby back to the girl's daddy's house. He has them held up with a gun pointed at them. He wants ten thousand dollars and some journal."

We quickly filled Dullie in on the journal's information.

"No wonder he's demanding the journal; he knows it's his ticket back to jail.

"What is he threating?" Josh asked Dullie.

"If we don't show up in two hours with the money and the journal, he will kill the baby. If we don't show up an hour after that, he will kill Susan's daddy. After that, he will kill Susan. From the sound of his voice, he meant business."

We were all stunned.

"We have to give him what he wants!" Tim declared.

"We ain't giving him what he wants, but we'll let him think we are," Dullie answered sternly.

As the three men were planning how to handle the horrible situation, the phone rang.

I answered it. It was Susan. She was crying hysterically!

"He's dead, he's dead!" she cried.

"Who's dead?" I demanded.

Upon hearing my, words the three men gathered around me.

"Alexander is dead!" Susan screamed.

"We will be right there, don't move!" I ordered.

We raced to Susan's father's house. Susan's daddy was dragging what appeared to be a body wrapped in a sheet to the edge of the road. After a good hour of hashing over what had happened, it seemed when Susan's big, burly daddy overheard the conversation between Jenkins and Dullie, he got steaming mad! He had lost all the fear of the gun in his face. He tackled puny Jenkins. The gun had fired and hit Jenkins right in the chest, an accidental self- inflicted shot to the chest.

At least, these were the facts concluded in police report.

Because of the horrible things Al Jenkins was saying, Clayton realized his daughter was more of a victim than he had thought.

Evie

Susan was sobbing. Her father held her with one arm and held baby Paul with the other.

Clayton looked over at the corpse and said, "I got back what you tried to steal, Jenkins. Now you get to meet your Maker and go straight to hell!"

He then looked at Susan, "May we never speak his name from our lips again."

With his family in his arms, Clayton limped back to his home with a simple nod in our direction.

There was no funeral for Al Jenkins. However, there was a burial. I went because I wanted to see him lowered to the ground with my own eyes.

Brother John and Beth had just arrived last week to pastor the church. To everyone's surprise, Brother John requested to say a few words at the burial. He asked Susan and her father to please attend. He said it would help them heal from this terrible experience. To my surprise, they showed up. Susan was carrying Paul. Clayton, Susan's father, looked like he had just showed up from the field. He was wearing dirty overalls.

He looked at me and said, "I want to see dirt piled up high over the Son of Satan."

I nodded my head in understanding, more than he knew.

Dr. Hamilton was there, along with the entire Anderson family. Grandpa even surprised me by being there. I feel he too wanted the chapter closed by seeing Al Jenkins put in a place where he could no longer hurt anyone.

Brother John began: "Thank you all for coming to witness this burial. In most situations like this, we talk about the deceased person in a positive way. We recall all the wonderful traits this person might have had. I encourage you to look around: there is no one among us who is family or friend of Robert Sucadas a.k.a. Mr. Alexander Jenkins. If I am not mistaken, there is no one who could speak kindly of him. Knowing all this causes a certain emotion to rise up in me. I feel sorrow; yes, ladies and gentlemen, I feel sorry for Mr. Alexander Jenkins."

As Brother John finished these words, Clayton stood up to leave, saying he could not sit here and hear how anyone could feel sorry for Jenkins. Brother John raised his voice louder than I ever believed it could get.

"Please! All remain seated and allow me to explain!"

"Daddy, please don't leave," Susan begged. "I want us both to hear what Brother John has to say."

Clayton sat back down with a frown on his face. He crossed his arms over his chest.

Brother John continued: "Alexander was once an innocent baby. He went from a baby to an innocent toddler, then to a young lad. What went wrong in his life to cause him to be so unloved, and so unloving? We may never know. It is true Alexander performed many unspeakable acts. He has hurt many of you. For some he has left scars. The scars run deep. You see and feel them every day. Therefore, Al Jenkins has power over you. Even from the grave, he is able to cause distress and pain. I am here today to suggest to you a way you can get rid of those scars and the pain forever. It's called forgiveness."

Susan's father made a grunting sound and stood up waving his finger and shouted, "Don't you dare tell me to forgive this snake. You don't know what he did to my daughter!"

"Daddy, please?" Susan begged.

Clayton looked at his daughter and, surprisingly, sat back down.

"Brothers and sisters, we have to forgive this man. Forgive, not for Alexander Jenkins because, yes, he is undeserving. Forgive for yourself. If you have a hard time with this, it helps to think of him as a child of God who went astray.

Shall we pray: Lord, please help us all to forgive this man for all the terrible things he has done and for all the pain he has caused. Lord, I know within myself I cannot forgive, but with your help I can forgive, and with forgiveness I will have freedom and healing. Lord, please help my brothers and sisters to receive this freedom and healing. In Jesus' mighty name, we pray. Amen.

"Ladies and Gentlemen, you are dismissed from this burial. But before you leave, if you truly desire to forgive this man, for your own sake, I have a request of you. Here beside me I have a basket of white roses; I ask you take a rose and lay it upon his grave. I will be the first to do so."

Brother John took a rose, knelt down on Al Jenkins grave, bowed his head in prayer, and laid the rose down. I felt a strong nudging to do the same. I have felt this nudging before, a nudging from God.

I walked up to the rose basket and took a rose in my hand. As I grabbed a rose, a thorn pricked my finger.

"Ouch!"

The prick was pretty bad. I noticed blood trickling down my hand.

I lay the rose down and whispered, "I forgive you Alexander Jenkins."

Evie

The rose was sprinkled with my blood. I rose to walk away, but before I did, I mouthed a final word:

"Checkmate."

Epilogue

Everyone at the burial put a rose down. Even Susan's daddy threw one down on the grave.

Grandpa decided his place was with me, so he and Poker moved in. He took Mama and Daddy's old room. I moved back into my room. Grandpa moving here made me so happy. I feel I have a family once again.

Susan moved back in with her daddy. Her daddy loves being a grandpa to Paul, who looks just like him. Tim asked Susan's daddy if he could court Susan.

He answered, "I reckon."

Josh and I are still courting. I am in no hurry to get married; I'm still young. Dullie has bets all over town. He bets we get married before the year is over.

Our pie business is still going strong. If it grows any bigger, we may have to open a restaurant in town. Grandpa offered to put up the money; he is tired of pies taking over the house. Poker loves it; we cook him up his own special crust.

Evie

Brother John and Beth love the town and the church, and we love them. Beth just gave birth to a baby girl. They named her Evelyn. They said they named her after someone who loved the Lord with all her heart and had strong character. This made me happy to be me.

PEGGY DILLEY

From the author

A heartfelt thank you to my readers. Thank you for going alongside Evie on her journey of freedom and forgiveness. Evie was birthed several years ago. I still remember where I was when the first paragraph came to my heart and mind. I was sitting on our patio; it was early spring, and my imagination took me to the year of 1946.

"It was 1946, after the war. Times were hard for everybody. We didn't have it as hard as some though; we only had three mouths to feed-Daddy, Mama, and me."

From that first paragraph the story of Evie flowed from my pen. It was as if the story wrote itself.

If there is a lesson to be learned from the story of Evie it is that of forgiveness. Forgiving those who have wronged us, frees us to love. It frees us to love ourselves and others. May God bless you today and everyday forward.

I would love to hear from you!

You can contact me at: **peggy@peggydilley.com**

or visit my website: **www.peggydilley.com**

to find out more about Evie and future projects. Please recommend this book to your friends and leave a positive review wherever you purchased this book.

Made in the USA
Columbia, SC
14 October 2021